Forthcoming by
Evangeline Ivers

A Court for Owls
Woods End
Soliloquoy

The Wall

The Wall

a tale by

Evangeline Ivers

A Woodbridge Book
1997

For the Children

*James William Howe, the narrator of this
tale, is a figment of my imagination.
But his story is truer than true.*

Evangeline Ivers
1997

Contents

Foreword

In Old Bell Falls, winters are cold, summers are short, the rocky soil unyielding. We who love the beauty of the place—the green valleys, the rolling hills, the swift streams, the sharp clear air— must come to terms. We, the hardy ones who remain, are heirs of stern traditions. Traditions of hard work and sacrifice, of hospitality (though reserved), of aid in times of need, of rectitude, and caring for one's own. And traditions as well (it cannot be denied) of judgment, and of pride.

Equal to the land, we are stubborn. Stubborn in virtue . . . and stubborn in vice.

Thus shaped by the landscape, I grew up. And more particularly was I, James William Howe, tutored by a certain feature of that landscape. Not natural, not placed by an act of God, but an addition, man made. A boundary set in place a hundred years after the founding of our town and nearly a hundred years before my birth (neatly dividing history in two): My Great-Grandfather Ephraim's Wall.

In winter, the wall was a graceful crest in the snow, snaking its way down from the edge of the woods above the high pasture, through the meadow, and out to the edge of the pond.

In summer it was just a darned old rock wall which we Howes (no help from the Meads on the other side) must tend.

Even as children, however, tending the wall with much complaint, we knew it was more than a mere pile of crumbling stones. It was a monument to the greater mystery dividing Howe and Mead. And, though we could not comprehend it, we were under its spell.

Thus enmity passed from generation to generation as a thief, stealing our affections. Greedy for our peace.

Sacrifice

*H*e was dead, that boy, when they pulled him from the dark cold waters of Abnak Pond. Still. Blue. Not a breath, not a flutter. Ten years old, a mother's only son, dead on Christmas Eve.

I saw it, not much past ten years old myself, dripping wet, my clothes turning ice against my skin, my feet and hands disappearing in the cold, my heart hot from fear and sorrow and guilt.

How he came to be lying there with folks all around him in a panic, shouting to one another over the sound of church bells wrung from their joyous pealing to the lead-dull toll of alarm . . .

How he came to be there in the snow with folks huddling over him, my father—ice forming in his dark wet hair, snow falling upon his broad strong back—pushing to move the water from his lungs, the others rubbing him, giving up their coats, in vain, to warm him, and then just plain giving up . . . .

How he came to be there . . . was more than I could bear to know.

Just boys we were, full of mischief and high spirits, acting our parts in the drama to which we were born. Reckless, foolish, not meaning to be cruel . . . not exactly.

Live! I cried in my mind, watching the closed eyes, black against the blue-white skin. *It was only a game! Please live!*

But no will of mine could conquer time, no will of mine turn back this horror. I wanted to run away, far and fast, to a place where this had not happened.

But I was frozen, doomed to watch as my father fought to undo what I had done.

It isn't fair! I cried in my heart. *Where are the others, more guilty than I! Why am I alone condemned to see?*

Up from the pond blew a sudden gust. A shiver of dread swept the congregation.

Don't give up! I prayed, thinking to promise my life for his.

Through the swirl of snow I saw my father fall

back, exhausted, defeated, the small form lifeless at his knees.

"No!" I cried aloud, my heart breaking.

And now, with my cry, another!

From up on the hill, a cry from a depth of pain that sliced me as it silenced the night. As if commanded, the townsfolk gave way at the sound, melting back as she passed through, white clothes streaming behind her in the storm, crying out his name.

And now, there was will enough . . . .

Friends

He was a Mead, is who he was. Gamaliel Stethington-Mead. For a Howe, such as I, all you needed to know about a person to call him foe was to know he was a Mead. And the feelings, we could be sure, would be returned in kind.

For as long as anyone could remember, it had been so. Unquestioned. Though charity and brotherhood were ever preached in the pulpit on Birchwood Hill, though kindness and generosity were fostered at every hearth, the rift between Howe and Mead possessed a morality of its own. Indeed, for a Howe to scorn a Mead was almost . . . virtue.

It was not always so between our two founding families of peaceful Old Bell Falls. Once upon a time, it was altogether different. And how it once was, must be the real beginning of my tale.

~

On a crisp October morning in 1844, almost a hundred years before Gamaliel Stethington-Mead went into Abnak Pond, two infant boys were brought to the white-wood church on Birchwood Hill—the newborn sons of Erastus Howe, the Bell Falls blacksmith, and Jeremiah Mead, the village cooper.

Carried in their mothers' arms, under the pealing of the bells their forefathers had forged, Nathaniel Mead and Ephraim Howe were christened on the self-same day.

They grew up together, sons of the green mountains, learning their fathers' trades, working the rocky soil, tapping the maples, tending sheep in the common pasture on the hillsides above Abnak Pond.

Happy and free, they roamed the hills and meadows where once Abnaki hunters faced the ruthless Mohawk, fishing the streams, scouting for game. As had their fathers before them, they pledged blood-brotherhood, as if warriors of ancient legend, vowing aid and loyalty for life. Defending their flocks on the rocky hillsides, they dreamed of adventure, and the bright future they would make together.

In the schoolhouse they conspired: If Nathaniel was quick at the books, deft with pen and ink, chalk and slate, Ephraim was champion of the playground, master of stick-pull and tug-of-war. If Nathaniel brought Ephraim through arithmetic and spelling bee, Ephraim was Nathaniel's defender in the yard.

Binding them further still was the friendship of their mothers—Miriam Smith Howe, descended on both sides from Bell Falls Founders, and Sophronia Wheelwright Mead, formerly (and still, in her emotions) of Springfield, Massachusetts, well-bred daughter of a textile magnate.

These two women, respected in all Bell Falls for superior qualities of heart, hand, and mind, imparted refinements to their sons, manners and matters suiting the most fortunate of city boys. So that every girl (and every girl's mother) in the valley had an eye upon the one or the other.

The boys grew up heedless of such attachments, regularly admitting into their company only two females: the baker's daughter, Rebecca DeVries, whose good sense (and never ending supply of fresh mince pies) were a welcome accompaniment to any expedition; and her friend, tidy little Marguerite LaPointe, whose father owned the general store.

If Marguerite lacked Rebecca's sturdy amiability, this was redeemed by the fact that, as early as age six, Marguerite was a reliable thief, and the ruffles of her ever-fresh starched pinafores yielded a limitless supply of exotic sweets purloined from the barrels in her father's store.

The boys' mothers differed dramatically in their opinions of these associations.

Sophronia Mead endured life in Bell Falls in the grand house which Jeremiah (aided considerably by her father's money) built for her at the end of Main Street, on the choicest remaining parcel of Mead family land, once designated for the railway depot. But Sophronia had no interest in her son's attachments in the place of his birth, for he, of course, would be making his future elsewhere.

Miriam Howe, on the other hand, was happy in the notion that her son would follow in the footsteps of his father, and in Rebecca DeVries she saw her own younger self. Sensible, intelligent, attractive without a threatening beauty, a suitable match for a hardworking country gentleman such as Ephraim would become.

Which fact Miriam mentioned to Sophronia over the needlework—pillow covers for Sophronia's new fainting couch, blue peacocks worked into mauve silk.

"Perhaps Ephraim will have plans of his own,

Miriam," Sophronia murmured, pulling a stitch. "I know I would never make such plans for Nathaniel."

"Of course not, Sophronia," Miriam smiled. "And please know that I do not mean to suggest that I see you in Marguerite LaPointe."

"I am happy to hear it, dear."

In no time at all, the friends' childhoods were over. In the same year that Marguerite was sent off to school in Boston, Rebecca, upon the death of her mother, assumed both the care of her family and her mother's role in the bakery.

As for Ephraim and Nathaniel, there was always plenty of hard work demanded of strong young men in Bell Falls. All that anyone could do, and more.

When news of the Union defeat at Fredericksburg reached town in December of 1862, the boys had just passed their eighteenth birthdays. They were adventurers after all, and, infused with a sudden patriotism, they determined to go to war.

Through the winter they prepared, and in spring, cheerfully deaf to all paternal admonitions and blind to maternal tears, Ephraim and Nathaniel set off to find General Hooker's forces in Virginia.

Of the emotions of this moment, Miriam Howe wrote, "My grief at my son's undertaking this monstrous, wasteful task is beyond my power to express. As for Sophronia, she cannot be consoled."

By the time the boys had crossed the border from New York into Pennsylvania, they had learned of Hooker's defeat at Chancellorsville, and of General Lee's advance up the Shenandoah Valley.

Invigorated by fresh indignation, they rode on, following instinct and rumor until on a muggy summer morning they heard sound like distant thunder, and, looking toward it, saw smoke rising faraway and faint.

Bright with ignorance and heedless courage, they rode towards the battle, until the sounds of the steady cannonade deafened them, the thickening smoke burned their lungs, and the stench of blood and death hit their bellies.

As if awakening, they beheld their destination— fields littered with men and horses in the agonies of dying. Everywhere, moaning and confusion. And ahead, along the crest of the hill, a mighty line of soldiers, behind rock and breastworks, poised to fire.

This, then, was war.

They tethered their horses to an oak, well away from the chaos, and began to walk across the fields towards the battle. In a moment, the cannoade ceased, and in the silence, a voice, far off but clear: "Forward, guide center! March!" And then the grand explosion, as the line opened fire on thousands upon thousands of men in gray emerging from the farther woods, advancing down the ridge, across the open fields, and up the rise directly into the Union center.

In horror Nathaniel and Ephraim watched as men fell, rank after rank, their fellows stepping over them, or upon them, in the senseless advance to certain death.

Suddenly, Nathaniel felt a blow, like grief. The sun failed. In darkness, he fell, Ephraim catching him before his head could strike the ground. Lifting him over his shoulder, Ephraim turned, striding through the bloody fields, Nathaniel's own blood oozing from his wound to run a slow stream down Ephraim's back.

Steadily, Ephraim walked, until he reached the oak where the horses waited, and there he laid his friend, unconscious, upon the damp grass. Carefully, he tore back the shirt to examine the wound. "Not too deep, thank God," he said. The ball, lodged inches from Nathaniel's heart, in muscle, not in bone, had been slowed by the thick leather vest which Sophronia had coerced upon her son.

From his pack, Ephraim took the supplies which his mother had sent. Kneeling again, he dug the shot and the bits of cloth and leather from the flesh, treated the wound with nettle, rum, and comfrey, and finally, with a broad strip of muslin he bound Nathaniel's chest.

Then he closed his eyes, and prayed.

Nathaniel awoke in the humid night, the summer moon floating in the sky. He felt submerged in the heavy air, his chest and arms on fire.

"Home, Ephraim," Nathaniel whispered, closing his eyes against the pain. "Home."

Marguerite

Reunited with the green hills, purged of the lure of adventure, Nathaniel Mead and Ephraim Howe undertook a task no one before them had attempted—the clearing of the hilltop woodland high above Abnak Pond, land their grandfathers had shared, but too rocky for anyone to covet.

They worked for an entire season, felling trees, prying stones. Times were changing, they considered. Sheep were not profitable enough. Here, they would grow thick wheatgrass, to feed a dairy herd.

For their industry, the young men were awarded, by the unanimous consent of their kin, an astonishing inheritance—not only the land they had cleared, but also joint possession of all property belonging to Howe and Mead, from the falls on the river, right up to the edge of the forest, with perpetual stewardship of Abnak Pond.

Expert with saw and axe, lathe and forge, Ephraim Howe and Nathaniel Mead assumed their stewardship with energy, raising two stone houses, wooden porches wide, secure and neat on opposite sides of the pond. Far enough apart, they would jest, for good relations, but both with a view of the river, of the sloping meadows of their childhood play, and of the sawmill on the falls.

In little more than a year, their work was complete. Twenty years old and already well proven in the world of men, they loaded their worldly goods into wagons, bade farewell to town, to father's rule and mother's care, and set their faces towards the morning sun.

Settled in upon either side of Abnak Pond, they made refinements: Ephraim built a milk house, dug a root cellar, shod his horse, while Nathaniel put up shelves for his books, and fashioned himself a desk and a reading chair.

The Autumn Sun shone approval upon Industry and Harmony in Old Bell Falls. Two young friends considered: Time for a man to make a choice.

Time now, they judged, to lift the eyes and look around, and perhaps, under the Harvest Moon, to commence the courting.

Miriam Howe learned of the plans on a visit out to her son, bearing fresh apple pie. She was welcomed by Nathaniel, skimming cream in Ephraim's kitchen.

"Ah, Auntie Miriam!" Nathaniel exclaimed, relieving her of the dish and bearing it to the table, while Ephraim fetched the plates. "Nothing in the world like one of your pies!"

"Would you like me to beat some of that cream you have skimmed off?" Miriam smiled. "Do you have sugar, Ephraim?"

"I say, Auntie M, did Ephraim tell you he is thinking of marrying?" Nathaniel teased, cutting himself a piece of pie.

"Well, I—!" Miriam brought a hand to her heart.

"Nathaniel is jesting, Mother. I have no one in mind." And Ephraim took for himself an even larger piece of pie.

"Can you call to memory my young cousin from Springfield, Ephraim?" wondered Nathaniel, straddling a chair at the kitchen table, spoon in the air and a twinkle in his eye. "The one with the flaxen hair?" And he took a mouthful of pie.

"Why, Nathaniel, she can not be more than fourteen years old!"

Nathaniel swallowed his pie with a cheery shake of the head. "Nearer eighteen by now, I should think. You do remember her, then?"

"I do," admitted Ephraim. "And I seem to remember her rather fetching friend, as well."

"Just so!" returned Nathaniel, once again lifting his spoon, and turning towards Ephraim's mother, who was needlessly beating the cream. "How can we thank you enough, Dear Aunt Miriam, for this most excellent gift!"

Miriam might have replied, but her son was musing aloud: "Her hair was auburn, I believe."

Nathaniel smiled. "Shall we saddle the horses, then, Ephraim. As soon as you have finished your pie?" He gazed, as if in the dreamy distance. "For methinks I disremember the color of her eyes."

But the journey that Miriam feared, the journey that could infect her son with discontent and lead him from his inheritance, would not be undertaken.

For, timely enough, another destiny intervened: In the sudden return of Marguerite LaPointe.

Old Bells Falls had never been kingdom enough for her. A vision of dark brown ringlets in white satin ribbons, of violet eyes under a bonnet's shade, of fresh-starched eyelet pinafore sailing in the swing under the Great Elm in the center square.

The damp wooden schoolhouse could never contain her. She was ever too clever, too splendid, too fine. Reading aloud the poems of Mr. Longfellow (brown ringlets falling along her cheeks), her voice was transportation to another realm.

Behind the counter in her father's store, an angel in ruffles and lace dispensing maple candy, she made a boy feel ashamed of his homespun clothes, and his callused hands, all the while he thanked heaven for her regard.

"Spoiled," Nathaniel Mead would mutter, while Ephraim Howe held his breath.

At fourteen, she had gone away to be "finished." At eighteen, she had returned.

They caught sight of her as they lingered outside the bakery, eating mince tarts fresh from the oven. Together, they watched, Ephraim and Nathaniel brushing crumbs from their jackets, Rebecca pushing back a wisp of hair from her forehead, wiping her hands on her floury apron, as the carriage brought Marguerite in from the train.

They watched as the coach traveled Main Street, pulling up at the General Store, watched her step lightly down, slim ankle buttoned in black leather, taking her father's hand.

The sight took Ephraim's breath. Those slender fingers so dainty in lace glove! That tiny waist a man's two hands could span! Those raven ringlets against the snow-white cheeks! A look in those eyes and a manner to set the heart aflame!

"Spoiled," murmured Nathaniel Mead.

She looked up to see them regarding her from across the street. Her face lit, and her violet eyes shone.

"Oh!" she exclaimed, one hand holding her hat to her head, the other hand gathering her skirts. "Look at you all! Oh, my! Oh, how good to see you!"

Carefully, whilst the three stood mesmerized on the bakery steps, Marguerite crossed the rutted road to reach them.

"My goodness, I would scarcely have recognized you boys!" she exclaimed. "My, my, my how you have grown up! Veritable men, aren't you now!" And she parted them to reach her flour-dusted bosom friend.

"Becky, darling!" the Finished One exclaimed, turning to offer a perfect cheek.

Dutifully, Rebecca leaned forward to leave a kiss (and a nose print of flour) upon the rouge.

Now the Finished One sighed, turning away. "Forgive me, but one really must rest from the journey. I see that Father's business is concluded, and we shall be going along home now. Please come later, Rebecca dear. For tea. *Chez nous.*" (At which Nathaniel rolled his eyes.) "I have so much to tell you about the city, dearest! *À bientôt!*"

But before Marguerite's dainty foot had reached the dusty Main Street of Quaint Little Old Bell Falls, Rebecca DeVries had retreated into the bakery, where there was always much work to be done.

She must have taken the meaning of his visits, awkward, to her father's store, too frequent, for this and for that, heedless of those who would judge him a fool.

She must have borne her father's jests, her mother's mild alarm, peeking through the parlor curtains at the blushing young man, the blacksmith's son, pacing to and fro along the white picket fence, pausing every now and then to linger, cap in hand, at the gate. His attentions must have touched her, for she was gracious, by all accounts.

Did he expect an invitation to tea, the day she came down the walk? Did he wait, heart pounding as she strode toward him, for the welcoming sound of her voice?

How could he have known, wringing his cap as she stopped, smiling, before him, what lay behind her sudden appearing? What mercy, what intention.

"Good-day to you, Ephraim!" (She carried a leatherbound volume under her arm.)

"Good-day, Marguerite." (His soft wool cap was damp in his hands.)

"I wouldn't want to trouble you, Ephraim," she smiled.

"No trouble . . . anything . . . I mean—"

"I was wondering . . . could you carry this out to Nathaniel?" She smiled again, extending the book. "He so rarely comes into town." She turned, ever so slightly, away. "It isn't a gift, mind you. . . . Merely a loan."

For a moment (while his heart stopped), her eyes searched the clouds. "He was always fond of Dickens," she said to the sky. "Even as a boy."

Silent, he took the book from her perfect, slender white hand, and, bearing the leatherbound burden under his arm, Ephraim Howe turned for home.

While Marguerite LaPointe, flushed from her success, hurried to confide her design to her dear Rebecca.

Out from town he trudged, along paths ablaze with autumn, through fields ready for harvest, across the languishing meadow (the noisy geese lighting upon Abnak Pond), along to Nathaniel's side.

"*She* sent it," Ephraim said, reaching his destination at last, extending the book to Nathaniel standing on the mill-fresh porch of his new stone house. "She asked me to bring it, to you."

Gladly, Nathaniel received the book, fingering the fine leather, ignorant that his lifelong friend was bidding him farewell in his heart.

"*A Tale of Two Cities*," Nathaniel smiled, as if he had been waiting.

For all Nathaniel was aware, Ephraim didn't care a fig anymore about Marguerite LaPointe. Not truly. What would a boisterous fellow like Ephraim do, after all, with a frail parlor violet such as she? A man of unfailing common sense, Ephraim must understand that she was no fit companion for a man determined to live by the sweat of his brow and the strength of his back.

For the exquisite Marguerite (spoiled indeed!) lived not on the crude cold earth, but in the realm of genteel imagination, where life transpired serene. As in a Boston parlor, where a gentleman (lately of Harvard) read and thought and spoke, and a lady (with a maid for the heavy work) took her leisure in silk, and her tea in fine painted porcelain. (What good those delicate lace-gloved hands for butter churn or milking pail?)

Thus settled in his secret mind, Nathaniel began to contemplate a secret dream, of another life, perhaps in another place.

This dream at first did not necessarily include an earnest fancy for Marguerite LaPointe (spoiled, after all). She was at first perhaps only a distraction, a token, an emblem of a rite of passage, as Nathaniel searched for who he was, apart from all he had known, for the first time admitting to consciousness his discontent in Old Bell Falls. By tolerating Marguerite's infatuaion with him, Nathaniel could try on a role, and perhaps at the same time save Ephraim from complete humiliation.

In such a mind, Nathaniel Mead permitted himself to be welcomed into the warm glowing parlor of The Family LaPointe.

While, at the edge of the woods beyond the high pasture, Ephraim commenced the wall.

He worked through the autumn, harvesting stones from the willing ground, worked past Thanksgiving, prying stones from the frosting earth, and on through the early winter snows, hauling stones from the pile they had cleared together to make pasture for their herd.

Never mind that an impartial observer might judge that Ephraim's careful wall lay a good two rods too far to the east, snaking out a healthy parcel of what might well be seen as Nathaniel's land.

No boundary had ever been drawn, no division ever contemplated at all. And, while a number of Meads took careful exception, and a spattering of Howes wondered how it might end, Nathaniel himself paid no more heed to Ephraim's gesture than he did to his mother's tears.

If he had grown to be truly fond of Marguerite, it was nothing to be ashamed of. She had many fine qualities, after all, apart from her exceptional beauty. Her Boston education had quite broadened her, and her company, Nathaniel found, was really quite . . . stimulating.

As for Ephraim's continued insistence upon taking offense, in Nathaniel's mind, Ephraim was a part of himself. No offense or division between them could last, once Ephraim regained his senses and swallowed his wounded pride.

As for his mother, Nathaniel trusted that she would soon learn, her prejudices overcome, that his Intended was the true lady she had always wanted for him, after all.

Thoughts full of future and of Marguerite LaPointe, Nathaniel Mead was content.

For all Ephraim's diligence, the wall had reached only the crest of the slope by Christmas, when the betrothal was announced, with the marriage proposed for the spring.

Landscape

Winter time in Old Bell Falls was always what you might call perfect: Blankets of pure white snow rolling over hill and dale, cloaking the evergreens, frosting the bare black branches, sparkling in the sun, glistening under the deep blue midnight sky.

At the falls below ice-locked Abnak Pond, a crystal marvel: frozen rainbows spread over slick black rock, the deep current piercing through glass to plunge, deafening, into the bottomless pool no winter's cold could ever tame, and emerging, rushing on, a fluid ribbon slicing silver through the frozen meadows, carving slick around the knoll, sliding under the bridge at the foot of Birchwood Hill, and slipping on to the valleys below.

All through the season, sleighs gliding swift on their runners, to the rhythm of sleigh bells, horses blustering, frosting the air. Sledders speeding down the hillsides (toboggans for the bold). Skaters streaking the pond (Don't go too near the falls!), warming at bonfires along the shore.

In the snug stone houses of the hillside farms, families gathered after evening chores, grateful for the harvest, settling in for the long cold winter. Bathed in fragrance of hot cinnamon-cider (apples fresh from the press), laced with the smells of baking bread, popping corn, mincemeat, hearty soup, they gathered close around the hearth, to read from the Good Book, from *Pilgrim's Progress*, and the works of Mr. Dickens.

In the center of town, neat painted houses glowed. Behind the frost-laced glass, in warm parlors, tea and cakes were served with grace, dinner spread on the crisp linen cloth, fine china, framed with gleaming silver. Succulence of goose, tang of steamed plum pudding. The latest tunes sung to the accompaniment of concertina—*"Sweet Adeline," "In the Evening by the Moonlight," "Daisy, Daisy, give me your answer, do . . ."* At the close of evening, a hymn—*"Lord of all, to thee we raise, this our song of grateful praise. Amen."*

Thanks given, the season deepened into the most hallowed time of the year.

Around the hillside hearths, families gathered to read of the Holy Babe. In the General Store, oak barrels brimmed with holiday delights: bon-bons, spices, sugarplums, walnuts, jellies, cranberries from Cape Cod. And spilling from the shelves, festive cloth, fancy hats, beads and tinsel, toys of wood and tin.

Upon the commons before the courthouse, the great blue spruce, magnificent in any season, was ringed with candles for Christmas Eve. High over the white-wood church on Birchwood Hill, the bells in the tower rang out peace, good will toward men.

~

Alone at his wall on Christmas Eve, Ephraim Howe heard the summons of the bells: *"O come, all ye faithful, joyful and triumphant!"* From the valley farms and the glowing streets of town, the folk of Old Bell Falls obeyed (*"O come, let us adore Him!"*), all streaming toward the church on Birchwood Hill.

Alone in his heart, Ephraim watched them go, as if they moved in another world, where love and faith yet survived. Alone, under the distant stars, lit by the silent white-cold moon, he watched all the people he had ever known, moving as one toward the church, to warm themselves in the celebration of light.

Numb, his bare hand resting upon cold stone, he watched . . . .

Until, down along the edge of the pond, a shadow caught his eye, and out from the shadow, a streak, a flash in the moonlight, a solitary skater, silver blades carving an arc on the ice. Free, ivory cape spread like wings, she sailed, until, turning abruptly, she carved her stop, spraying a cold crystal dare.

Swiftly, he followed, her slim dark lover, reaching for her hand.

But she was off, a night-bird flying. "Catch me!" she cried, her laughter flaunting her skill. Gliding, twirling, floating, she taunted him, and then, breaking from a figure-eight, she soared once more, sailing . . . too close to the falls!

"Stop!"

Their voices rang as one in the clear night air, Nathaniel's from the pond, Ephraim's from the wall.

"Stop, Marguerite! Come back!"

(How could she flirt with such danger!)

And as Nathaniel raced across the thinning ice toward her, Ephraim frantically plowed through snow.

The crack was the deep sound of doom, the end of the earth . . . .

It was Ephraim, always the stronger, who reached her first. Sliding in deep snow down the slope to the bank of the frigid stream, striking out into the treacherous current, swimming in ice, he seized her as she sank into the deep black pool beneath the pounding falls.

While upon the bank Nathaniel, crazed and frozen, sobbed on his knees, as if he wished he, too, could go under, and disappear into eternal night.

It was Ephraim who pulled her out, carried her in his arms—broken, still, the cold dark water streaming from the pale wool cape, streaming from the raven hair, the skate blades still bound to her feet, gleaming under the Christmas moon.

It was Ephraim who laid her on the snowy bank, working in vain to warm her, until Nathaniel, gasping, thrusting him aside, claimed his right to mourn her cold wet face with kisses.

For the first time since the church bells had been hoisted to the tower, they were silent on Christmas Day. The townsfolk abandoned their celebrations, to move solemnly down Main Street to the merchant's house, to pass through the crepe-draped parlor where Marguerite LaPointe lay still as ivory in a fine oak box crafted by the cooper, Jeremiah Mead.

Every citizen of Old Bell Falls passed through the parlor that day. Except for two who mourned beyond reason: Ephraim Howe, standing fast, knee-deep in snow at the river's edge, keeping vigil over the falls, and Nathaniel Mead, feverish at work with pick and shovel, under a great bare elm in the snow-filled churchyard on Birchwood Hill.

On the following day, under chill gray skies, the townsfolk gathered once more, as Pierre and Marie LaPointe surrendered their child to the frozen earth.

The New Year rang in and life resumed in Old Bell Falls, Marie LaPointe descended into her grief. Before the return of spring, she had joined her daughter under the great elm on the hill, leaving her husband to sell all he owned and to vanish into the depths of the northern woods.

Sophronia Mead, meanwhile, unable to console her only child, withdrew from the society she had always scorned. The grand house at the end of Main Street, once the self-appointed hub of Bell Falls cultural life, now darkened, curtains drawn.

Though Erastus Howe and Jeremiah Mead (themselves only distant kin, but lifelong brothers), entreated their sons to reconcile and return to the comforts of their companionship, and of their family dwellings in town, both young men refused. And on cold winter nights when others' windows blazed with the comfort of light, two stone houses stood dark and silent on either side of Abnak Pond, divided by a cold stone wall, steadfast in bitter grief.

By planting time, Nathaniel had abandoned his house and his share of the herd to the care of his grieving father, and he fled, to a life of wandering and study abroad.

Dogged, Ephraim remained, working dawn to dusk on his farm, and every spare moment on the wall, pausing only, from time to time, to tend an elm-shaded grave. But for the food his mother brought, he might have starved.

Miriam's life was now a frenzy of devotion to her husband and children, and to her Cousin Jeremiah and his stricken wife (for the remaining two years of Sophronia's life), drowning herself in works of charity, as if thereby to restore order to the world, and peace to her mind.

At last, Ephraim's wall reached the edge of the pond. His work was done. It only remained to plant two rows of sapling apple trees along the wall, on the strip of land that was rightfully his, no matter how the Meads might complain.

He must turn now to improving the house. A man, after all, must make a life.

In time, consenting to consolation, Ephraim took Rebecca DeVries to wife, presenting her on their wedding day with a rocking chair of choicest oak, the finest piece he had ever made.

Neighbors

When Nathaniel Mead suddenly reappeared one dark winter day with his scrawny little boy and his wife with the foreign name, no one was more surprised than Ephraim Howe.

"I never thought we'd see the likes of him again," he said, lifting an eyebrow and settling back into his warm chair by the fire. "Wouldn't even come for his own father's funeral."

For Jeremiah Mead, only the winter before, had contracted the fever. Having heard no word from his son in many years, he had willed the grand house on Main Street to the public use, as library and cultural center, to be administered by the Bell Falls Ladies League, in memory of Sophronia Wheelwright Mead.

At her husband's indifference to Nathaniel's return, Rebecca was dismayed. "I've heard tell they have nothing, Ephraim. Hardly anything at all to eat in that cold bare house. And we have plenty to spare."

"Let his books keep him warm," Ephraim groused.

Her bonnet already in hand, Rebecca regarded her husband. "Ephraim. Where is your charity."

"Let it be, Rebecca," he said to the fire. "Let it be."

But the bonnet was on, and Rebecca was off, her daughters compelled to the work, loading the provisions, hitching the horses, bundling the little boys into the sleigh.

In broad daylight they drove, the cold air biting their cheeks, around the pond on the packed snow trail, the runners smooth as glass. Around the pond and over the bridge, in defiance of Ephraim Howe. Over the bridge and up Meadside Way, the horses snorting mist.

The children trembled, wrapped in quilts, huddled in straw in the bed of the sleigh, as their mother drove the horses across the virgin snow, blazing a path to the silent house they had never dared near before.

The sleigh bells were a warning, carried on the frigid air, and as Rebecca reined the horses, a curtain fluttered at a window.

"Come, children," their mother commanded. "Carry the provisions to the porch! Be careful of loose boards!"

Many times before Rebecca's children had been bidden to such an errand of mercy, but never before had they performed it in fear.

Who was that at the window?

No one.

Do you hear something?

Nothing at all.

Quickly, they worked. Until two smoked hams, four loaves of fresh brown bread, a pumpkin, three winter squash, a pot of warm beans, and a bushel of bright red apples were secure on the weathered porch.

Then, squaring her shoulders, setting her bonnet straight, Rebecca approached the door, a basket on her arm. Lifting her hand to knock, she started as the door creaked open, rusty on its hinge.

For a moment, the sight of the fragile woman in the doorway—slender, dressed in flowing fabric, too thin for the damp winter air, the knitted shawl no protection from the cold . . .

For a moment, at the sight of this frail creature, and the dark-eyed boy clinging to her skirts, Rebecca was speechless. And speechless also was the object of her charity, who could only stare at this imposing visitor, and the bounties behind her on the porch.

At last, she found her voice: "I am Rebecca Howe, Mrs. Mead. I have come to welcome you to Bell Falls." And she was pleased to be received with a smile.

They might have been friends from that moment—timid Angela Mead and bold Rebecca Howe—but for the sudden appearance of Nathaniel at the door.

She met his eyes, and a world passed between them in the silence.

"It has been a long time, Nathaniel," she said at last.

"Indeed, Rebecca. It has." He stepped in front of his wife and son, as if to bar their view.

"You heard I married Ephraim. Some time ago."

"I did hear that," he conceded, making a careful reckoning of the goods laid on the porch, and of the solemn young faces at her heels.

"These are our children. Six of them. So far."

"A fine family, Rebecca. And a generous offering."

"I brought a pie," she said, extending the basket. "Still warm."

The briefest smile flickered across Nathaniel's face. "Is it . . . mince?"

"It is," Rebecca smiled back.

"Ah." (And, perhaps, thought Rebecca, a tear stood in his eye.) "Yes, well, it is certainly good to see you, Rebecca, and we are most grateful, but if you would just tell him that he needn't—"

"I come on my own, Nathaniel."

His face showed no emotion now, but the voice was colder than the air: "So. That's the way, is it."

"What I meant to say—"

"Thank you all the same, Rebecca, but we have no need."

And he retreated into the cold stone house, drawing with him his wife and son, the heavy door creaking shut.

For a moment, the square shoulders fell. Then, sighing deeply, she placed the pie-basket beside the pot of beans and turned to her children.

"Come, children," she said, taking the baby from her daughter Elspeth, who took brothers Luther and Ned by the hands. "We'll come back another day."

What five-year-old Luther Howe would remember of this day was watching that cold house retreat, all that food left there on the porch, and a sad little boy shut inside, who might never be his friend.

On Christmas morning, fleeing their father's ill humor, the Howe girls took their little brothers out to play fox-and-geese. They were witness then to an astonishing event—the new neighbor from Meadside, dragging a bushel basket on a sled, right up to the low rock wall. Witness to the shower of bright red apples, tumbling over the stones, shiny, onto the snow.

"Merry Christmas!" squealed little Ned Howe, enchanted at the sight.

"But they needed them," worried Luther, feeling a pain grow in his heart.

"Don't worry," Elspeth consoled. "They kept all of Mother's food."

Happy, the little ones scampered for the apples, tumbling in the snow.

But from the house, their father's voice sounded, stopping them in their tracks: "Let them rot there!"

And so they did.

Passing

What folks couldn't figure out, was why Nathaniel Mead had come back at all. And if now, why not sooner, when he might have been some comfort to his long-suffering father, and might have made claim to his mother's house in town.

So why? And why now? Certainly not for the creature comforts, holed up out there in that long-untended place. And not for the comforts of friends and family, for he hardly made an effort to renew old ties, and even rebuffed his kin.

Certainly not for profit. He made no move at all to recover his share of the dairy herd he had long ago abandoned. And he had never shown much inclination to work the land.

Had they been allowed, the folks of Bell Falls would have welcomed back this bright young son with open arms. And, being all of them proper Christians, they even would have accepted the Italian wife, had Nathaniel made any attempt to show her about.

But he didn't. He was so queer, and so standoffish, that almost everyone gave him up for a stranger. The only folks he ever spoke to were his cousin Tom and his boys, when they came to deliver the milk, and to young Stu Evans, who had taken over the general store.

Even on Sunday morning, when the whole valley answered the summons of the church bells on Birchwood Hill, Nathaniel Mead was perverse, driving out early with his wife and boy, to visit a fancy Roman church up north, where a number of her countrymen worked the quarries.

He had lost his mind, most folks concluded, though no one would mention how it might have begun. And if a shadowy figure was seen, from time to time in the dead of night, to haunt the willow grove near Abnak Pond, or the churchyard on Birchwood Hill, no one was ever *certain* it was Nathaniel Mead. Surely he was never seen in either place by light of day.

It must have been failure abroad that brought him back, they decided, to something undisputedly his. What had he been while he was away? A scholar? A teacher? Certainly nothing to broaden the chest or light the eye. Rumor had it he was writing a book!

What else he was up to, couldn't be guessed, though the postmaster (Ephraim's brother Isaac) let it slip that thick letters passed back and forth, involving a fancy address in New York.

What sustained the family, where it came from, the little cash they dispensed in town, no one could say. (Cousin Lucas Howe, who ran the bank, was the most tight-lipped man in town.) Perhaps, ran the speculation, the famous Wheelwrights of Springfield had deigned to settle something, after all, upon Sophronia's son.

And that book he was writing! What was it? What did it tell?

But Nathaniel Mead remained a mystery, a stranger in the place of his birth. And few others, perhaps only Rebecca Howe, ever made a real effort to heal the breach. Certainly, Ephraim himself did not.

If any doubt remained as to the soundness of Nathaniel's mind, it was dispelled by the mighty work he undertook the first spring after his return—to search out from the virgin woodlands fifty hemlock saplings, to plant a row along the wall.

The work at first seemed mere lunacy. Only later did its bitter design appear, as the hemlocks began to cast a morning shade upon Ephraim's apple trees.

Though few among Howe or Mead would presume to judge precisely where half met half in what once had been common ground, it seemed that, in Nathaniel's mind (as that mind had become), Ephraim had drawn a battle line.

A slow retribution, to be sure, a slow advance. But Nathaniel was content for now, his peculiar son Hiram at his side, to watch his hemlocks grow.

While from his side of the wall, young Luther Howe wondered if Hiram Mead would ever be his friend.

In the schoolyard, Hiram Mead suffered sorely. At running, jumping, and pulling sticks, he was no match for the strapping Howes, who called him a fancy boy, and worse.

The Mead boys, loyal to the family name, if not to their peculiar cousin, made half-hearted defense, which grew into a rift in the schoolyard, the bloodied noses and blackened eyes carrying the message home.

Now rancor emerged in Old Bell Falls that had never been seen before. Parents, Howe and Mead, under the weight of complaints from the exasperated schoolmarm, began to fling accusations of their own:

Whose boy did what to whom, and whose fault, and which parents were, after all, to blame. (What can you expect from a Howe? A lot more than you can expect from a Mead! You'll kindly step outside and say that again!)

All the while, inside the red schoolhouse, Hiram Mead worked his private revenge. With chalk and slate he had no equal, and he turned every spelling bee into a rout. His manner and wit made the teacher his slave, and he was ruthless in repartee.

The Meads fell back in awful pride. No thick-headed Howe was ever a match for this!

In spite of his ferocious kin, Luther Howe remained apart, watching, hoping the bad feelings would end.

"You must always stand for the right, Luther," his mother Rebecca had told him. "Even if you must stand alone."

And Luther tried, standing alone, even admiring (in secret) Hiram's skills. Until the day Luther lost the spelling bee (faltering upon *deceit*), and Hiram chose to gloat.

"Well, I'm real surprised you don't know *that* one, Luther," Hiram sneered, as Luther's face began to burn. "A Howe ought to know just about everything about deceit, I'd think." He stopped a moment, pretending to turn away. Luther's fists began to work.

"Say, Luther," Hiram sneered again, over his shoulder. "Why not bring the teacher an *apple*! It might help." Now Hiram started to laugh, like this was the funniest thing in the world. "'Course . . . she might not like **stolen goods**!"

In an instant, the tender spot hardened in Luther's heart. Where once was obedience to his mother's admonition, where once was even admiration, wrapped in a memory of a cold lonely boy clinging to his mother's skirts, was now a smoldering rage.

The drubbing that followed left Hiram bruised, but (so unfair!) it left Luther with the blame.

"Do not harm the weak, Luther!" Ephraim scolded, receiving the teacher's report.

"But he called us thieves, Father!" countered Luther, fighting tears.

At this, Ephraim bristled, rising from his chair to fill Luther's sight: "No Howe ever took anything he did not deserve!"

Cowering before his father's anger, Luther just missed being struck by the tin cup, flung against the chimney, its contents hissing upon the hearth.

When will it be finished? wondered Rebecca Howe, watching the poison spread to her son.

Initiation

Before the wall, before there had been any Howes or Meads in our neck of the woods at all, there had always been the falls. And, always, in the spring, the ritual of First Crossing.

It had begun with the native Abnak (or so the legend went): The passage of a boy into manhood, marked by his crossing of the river during the height of spring runoff, across the ledge through the falls, east to west. A treacherous undertaking that no parent could approve, though all must remain silent—a father having no doubt once made the journey himself, and a mother (for her son's sake) keeping from

~ 47 ~

her thoughts the knowledge that the passage was even more perilous than it appeared.

Each boy must judge for himself when he was ready, but must make the attempt at least by age siteen, if he wanted any respect at all.

Having taken his decision, the boy must present himself at the falls at the proper time, before the end of May, when the melting snows from the hills and upper valleys had brought Abnak Pond to brimming full, the water creeping into the willows along the banks, and spilling over the falls with such force that strength and skill and utmost care were required to maintain footing across the rocks.

The candidate must arrive before dawn, bringing with him such witnesses of friend and kin as he desired, who would range themselves on either side of the stream, above the falls and below, blankets and heavy ropes in hand, in the event of misadventure.

Not that real misfortune had ever occurred. The only failures were failures of nerve at the outset, when the shock of icy water over slippery rock could overwhelm a boy, no matter how accustomed he thought he was to the chill New England spring. What was called for then was to turn back, to try another day. Though such a failure might be disappointing for spectators looking for a thrill, it would not result in ridicule of him who failed. For, as everyone knew well enough, mishap in this undertaking could send a boy to great injury, and likely to his death.

It was not uncommon, then, for a boy to make a few false starts. Which was surely what everyone expected, when Luther Howe announced that he was ready, having only just turned thirteen.

The story had been told often enough, of how Luther's father Ephraim, in company with Nathaniel Mead, had made the passage in the spring of his fourteenth year, younger, as far as anyone could recall, than anyone had ever tried it before.

If Luther had not his father's size, he knew he had his strength. If his father (and Hiram's father!) could cross at thirteen, so could he! Something that puny Hiram could never, would never dare, do!

Well aware that his mother (honored tradition or not) would surely prevent him, Luther swore his companions to secrecy and set out a good while before dawn on the second day of May.

Word had made its way around, however, and when Luther Howe arrived at the falls, some dozen spectators had gathered to watch him, too young, risk life and limb.

From a safe vantage point below on the bridge, Hiram Mead was distant, disdainful witness. "Abnak legend, my foot! Some dumb farmer made this up, and I'd be hanged if I'd risk *my* neck!"

While, fortified by the power of new rage, Luther began his perilous journey.

There was, first of all, the need to find the way, in the pale end of night, inching with bare hands, and feet clad in wool socks for better purchase on the slippery rocks. Inching out, ankle deep, then in up to the knees, sidewards in the stream, braced against the ice-cold flow. Inching out to the center, and then, plunging through the frigid water-veil into blackness, finding chill shelter, gasping for breath, on the hidden ledge behind the plummeting falls.

Then, taking courage, in firm denial of the deep roiling pool far below, to move again, numb fingers searching with blind knowledge the way out through the icy veil. At last emerging, breathless, burning from the cold, moving only by effort of sheer will, yet cautious, feet leaden, over the black mossy rocks, slow journey in the pink morning light, back to safety, amidst the cheering on the shore.

As Luther Howe (youngest ever by half a year!) was cheered across the last chill stretch, Hiram Mead, skipping rocks with perfect skill from the bridge far below, was unimpressed. "If you're going to risk your life," he scowled, "it ought to pay."

At the sight of her triumphant, dripping son, borne home in victory by the youth of Old Bell Falls, Rebecca Howe dropped her ladle and brought her hand to her fainting heart.

While, beside her, just in from milking the cows, Ephraim Howe was stern: "Fool boy!" (But, behind his eyes, a smile.)

Homecoming

A dozen years, and Nathaniel's hemlock trees were tall enough. Under the long damp morning shade, Ephraim's apples began to rot. (On the Howe side of the wall, the axe was heavy in Luther's hands.)

While Hiram Mead, by age seventeen, was more than weary of Old Bell Falls, and of his reclusive father's earnest tutoring, to boot.

One bright day in June, wearing his fancy-boy suit and his customary smirk, Hiram, without a backward glance, left town for the morning train. Not bound for Hanover or Cambridge, however, to university as his father had intended, but to the bustling ports of Boston Town, to use his wits to make his way.

Alone with his weary wife, beyond a barrier of moldering apple and mournful hemlock split by a wall of crumbling stone, Nathaniel Mead passed his days.

Too soon, loneliness and grief and the chill damp climate took Angela Mead to a grave among the granite statues in the fancy churchyard up north.

When Ephraim Howe, not long thereafter, met a sudden shocking death at the sawmill, he had not spoken to Nathaniel Mead for nearly thirty years.

Informed of the tragedy—of how his old friend, a strong man yet in his prime, reaching too far to steady a beam, lost balance and fell, splitting his head on the sawmill floor—Nathaniel wept.

Too late, however.

Luther Howe, who had found his father dead, was inconsolable. He took to tramping the hills, stone-faced, silent, absent from Howeside for days on end.

Rebecca, weary in her grief and fearful for Luther, considered abandoning the farm altogether. The girls were married and settled in town. Ned was courting Caroline Carter in earnest, and would find his life's work on her father's newspaper. Enoch, she would apprentice to her brother in the bakery. She herself had been invited to daughter Elspeth's home, where grandchildren could occupy her time.

All was settled then. Except for Luther, the trouble in Rebecca's mind.

Luther must leave Bell Falls, she concluded. Choose a different life, clear his heart, his very soul, of the tragedies of Abnak Pond. Her son must leave his father's house, his father's work, must leave off the tending of the cold stone wall.

But Luther, returning from his tramping in the hills, was of another mind. Determined, he claimed his birthright: The stone house, the land, the moldering apple trees. The sawmill . . . and the wall.

As for Nathaniel Mead, what had been mere cantankerous isolation now became alarming eccentricity. Indulging a heretofore unknown interest in scientific experiment, he began receiving packages of unusual shape and size. Making the delivery from post-train out to Meadside, Cousin George Mead would shake his head.

From Howeside Luther took note: The noxious fumes carried on the clear air, the strange lights in the windows at night, the sudden explosions.

"He's trying to blow the place up," muttered Luther, at work with his brother Ned at a breach in the wall. "He's gone mad."

In his twenty-first year, already his own man, Luther Howe married Hannah Moore from over in Cooper's Glen, and in no time at all, posterity arrived.

My father, William Christian Howe, was born on the first Christmas Eve of the New Century, in the house his Grandfather Ephraim had built, overlooking Abnak Pond.

Hannah Howe, aglow with new motherhood and the spirit of the Holy Season, cradled her child in her arms, pronouncing his name, and making prophecy:

"He will be a blessing to us all," she declared. "An instrument of peace."

Luther smiled, receiving his firstborn son and turning to present the child to its grandmother, Rebecca.

"Would that it might be so!" whispered Rebecca Howe, wiping a tear. "Would that it might be so!"

~

Meanwhile, Hiram Mead was prospering from his Brownstone in Boston Town. First with the delivery of bottled milk, and then in the soft-drink trade.

He married a young woman from the city, a "theatrical," Rosalind O'Doule, whom he drove up from Springfield in his Haynes-Duryea motorcar, all dressed up in flounces and furs.

Watching them chug-chug down Main Street, on the way out to see the Old Man, Old Bell Falls took stock.

Hiram Mead, tall, dark, and smug under his waxed moustache, sat in command at the steering wheel, crowned in straw boater, trussed up in black frock coat, white vest, and striped trousers. (You could almost hear him crow!)

While Rosalind O'Doule sat in a pretty pout on the seat beside him, cinched into unnatural proportions, lace collar up to her ears, gauze-wrapped picture hat perched upon flaming hair piled at least a foot high, the hatpin the size of a sword!

On both sides of the Howe-Mead rift, tongues began to wag. A quiet Eye-talian woman, such as Hiram's mother had been, was one thing. A brazen, painted, city-Irish redhead was quite another!

They didn't come out to Bell Falls often, however. No matter how grand they tried to appear, a journey from Boston, or even Springfield, by motorcar over rutted roads, was not easy. They might never have come at all, but for Hiram's need to show off.

In time, there was a little girl, Victoria, after the good Protestant Queen, though she was christened by

Father O'Whatchamacallit of Saint Somethingorother in Boston, and she was, except for her coloring, the spitting image of Rosalind O'Doule.

Scarcely had Hiram's little Victoria captured her grandfather's heart, when that heart broke one last time, and Nathaniel Mead passed from this earth.

Ignorant of the current whereabouts of the elusive Hiram, the Mead kin reclaimed their own, and laid Nathaniel to rest, not in the popish churchyard where his foreign wife reposed, but with the rest of the Meads on Birchwood Hill, not fifty yards from Ephraim Howe, and nearer still to the elm-shadowed corner, and the long-neglected grave of Marguerite LaPointe.

Once more the stone house at Meadside stood empty. And it seemed as if it always had been so.

Until one spring day when Hiram Mead, the Fizzle Water King, appeared again in town, in a shiny black Model T, with rouged, feathered Rosalind beside him, and, perched in the rumble seat, nine-year-old Victoria, in green velvet dress and satin-rose-trimmed hat.

Right through town they drove, without a sidewise glance. Through town, around the knoll, past Birchwood Hill, along Church Lane to Old Trail Road, across the bridge below the falls, and on out to the farm, where dapper Hiram, it was rumored, planned a modest Country Retreat in the quaint little town of his youth.

~

William Christian Howe was ten years old when he first laid eyes on Victoria Mead, a city girl in satin roses, tossing pebbles into the pond.

Why he must hate her, having never even made her acquaintance, he was only vaguely aware. It had more to do, he knew, with something dark in the past than with this eyesore palace her father was building on the other side of the pond.

Bringing out a fancy architect from Boston, shipping the lumber and hardware in by train, hiring only

Meads to do the work, Hiram Mead was just plain foolish, at best pigheaded, because everyone knew the Howes were the best woodworking men, and the only decent masons and iron-workers, for fifty miles around.

But Will Howe wasn't inclined to pay any heed to the grownup whispers, to the sniggering about a genuine Mansion-of-Ill-Repute smack in the middle of Meadside Farm, with Madame Rosalind O'Doule at the door.

(When Will asked his mother what this meant, she merely scowled and fed him Castor Oil.)

It was a mansion, all right, with indoor plumbing throughout! Sixteen spacious rooms, of requirements precise, built onto the old stone house, which would be retained as summer kitchen. A carriage house, too, for the buggy and sleigh, with a compartment for the Touring Car. And in place of the old pump house, a genuine wishing well! (What next? A drawbridge and a moat?)

Obviously, ol' Hiram was clever, bragged the Meads.

No honest man made that much money that fast, knew Luther Howe.

While a slew of Meads set themselves to quick-learning the builders' trades, the Howes commenced to reinforce the wall.

When he could steal away, Will Howe would climb the tallest blighted apple tree, in hopes of catching sight of Victoria Mead through the hemlock hedge.

Sometimes he would see her alone in the meadow, twirling in a sea of Queen Anne's Lace, or gathering wildflowers, or plucking fiddleheads to strew an invisible path. Or he would watch her amble down to the pond, to stir her watery reflection with a stick, to listen for frogs, or speak to the geese.

Climbing down from the tree, inching closer (keeping well to his side of the wall), he would crave to hear what she said to the birds, crave to show her where to find fish, or to catch some polliwogs. Watching her shield her eyes and lift her gaze to the sky, he wondered what shapes she saw in the clouds. Did she see galleons and ponies and flocks of sheep? Or other things, beyond a country boy's imagination?

"Will's gone looney," his brother Gideon snickered to his brother Tim, at work on the wall.

After which Will took greater care to avoid observation, by his brothers and by Cousins Porter and Charlie, both about to be married, and both profane.

None of them could understand someone like the new girl from Meadside, he knew. She was almost magic, he thought as he watched her move along the edge of the pond, parting willows with her hands. She was like a girl in a story book that his mother might read to him by the fire. Even though he could see her clearly, hear the willows rustle as she moved by, she was very far away.

One day, she wandered farther, all the way down to the falls. He followed, almost hoping she would see him, not wanting to seem a spy.

Reaching the bank above the ledge where the pond began its spill, she stood a moment, watching.

Be careful! he wanted to warn her, knowing her feeling at the wonder, the attraction of the falls. Be careful! Don't fall in!

The falls were beautiful in any season, painting rainbows over the rocks. This spring Will had for the first time crossed them, all the way from Howeside to Meadside, alone, with no one to cheer him, no one to welcome him. But more important, no one to prevent him because he was too young.

Making his way over slick rock, icy water beating his face, he plunged, numb, through Center Falls to the hidden chamber behind, defying the cold, the pain, and the fear of the bottomless pool, where he could be sucked down, spinning forever, never to be heard from again.

But, having made his passage in secret, he finds now that he wants to tell. Not the others. But her, the stranger from Meadside.

He watched as she moved closer, to see the water, pulled by the force of the falls, make gentle swirling pools against the bank. He watched as she took courage, brushing her hair from her face, grabbing up her skirts, and moving along the bank, down toward the ledge. He watched, his heart in his throat as she dared move out to the edge, peering over, her face refreshed by the spray of water bent upon the craggy depths.

How far will she go? he wondered, afraid to speak, only praying she would not dare too far. If only he could stand beside her, reveal his daring, his knowledge of the treacherous way to the other side.

Suddenly, she startled, and quickly moved back from the edge, searching the bank with her eyes. And then, slowly, she went away.

Encounter

Steadily, the grand house rose on Meadside Farm. One story, two, then three. Bedecked with pillars, porches, trellises, gingerbread trim. The biggest house, and by far the prettiest, that Will Howe had ever seen.

In the middle of the second summer (just after the painters began to arrive), she spoke to him for the first time. Taken with watching her weave a daisy crown, he had forgotten himself, and walked out in plain sight.

"You're a Howe," she said suddenly, as if creating him on the spot.

"Will," he offered, surprised he could speak at all. She looked up from her work. "I am Victoria." "Yes." "Victoria Theodora Catherine Elizabeth Mead."

"They sure gave you a lot of names," he blinked.

"I added a few myself," she said, extending the daisy crown.

He stepped forward and reached out, accepting her gift with a bow. "William Christian Howe, at your service."

"How old are you, then, William Christian?" she asked, taking him in.

"Twelve this coming end of December. I was born on Christmas Eve."

"That makes you rather special," she observed. "You are awfully big for your age."

"I suppose so," he said. "How old are you?"

"I am ten, as of the past May twenty-fourth. I was

born on Queen Victoria's birthday. Hence, I am special, as well."

William could not recall ever having heard anyone else say *hence*, except when reading from a book.

"And I am the perfect size for my age."

"I guess you are," William smiled.

"My father says Howes are sneaky and stupid." (But still, in her eyes, a smile.) "Are *you?*"

"I don't think so. Anyway, you wouldn't want to hear what *my* father says about the Meads."

She set a ring of daisies upon her head. "Why don't you put on your crown, William Christian?" she said.

And so they were friends.

Or, they might have been. For, although the house was at last completed (Mead Mansion in Old Bell Falls), Hiram never brought his family out to stay.

There was only one brief blaze of glory in the new house on Meadside Farm, in December of 1912, when, done up like an English lord, Hiram Mead once again blew into town.

With Redhaired Rosalind (not quite an English lady) swathed in snow-white fur, poised upon the seat beside him, with Victoria (Theodora Catherine Elizabeth), chafed cheeks framed in the generous hood of her red-velvet cape, hands buried in her gray fur muff, enthroned on the rear-facing seat across,

Hiram was driven out to Meadside (bells a-jingle) in Cousin George Mead's two-horse sleigh.

Young Will Howe, in town for ginger and molasses, nearly fell off his horse at the sight.

On through December, the Hiram Meads were in residence, gracing the townsfolk with their fancy needs. A little this, a little that. Fetched from town in the two-horse sleigh.

Of course, the meager resources of Old Bell Falls could never meet all the needs, and for several weeks the furnishings and decorations and supplies packed in straw traveled from the train station out to Meadside by sled, long wagon, and carriage cab.

Carpets from Persia, lace curtains and linens from "Bruxelles," china from Limoges. Dutch tiles and vases, Tiffany lamps, British crystal, cutlery, sterling silver. Brass objects of exotic design. A frail fainting couch upholstered in red brocade, eight elegant Queen Anne arm chairs, a dining table, three tea tables, four chests, two armoires. Four, no five canopy beds. (Not good sturdy pieces of cherry or oak, such as a Howe might produce at the mill, but frivolous designs, of walnut and pine, fancied up with inlays and lacquers and veneers.) And if all this were not enough, there were garlands and tinsel, fireworks from China, and a Chickering grand piano for the parlor!

"Never knew there was such a market for Fizzle Water," Luther Howe was heard to remark.

Then, a week before Christmas, the food began to arrive. From beyond the wall, through the hemlocks, Will Howe and his brothers watched the ice house fill. With seafood—shrimps, lobsters, and crabs. Hams and turkeys and geese, and slabs of prime roast beef.

Sneaking over in the early morning to peek in through the windows of the old stone kitchen, the Howe boys saw the pantry fill with fruits and vegetables, tinned meats and great round wax-dipped cheeses, dark tall bottles with fancy printed labels. Shiny tins of exotic treats. And lots and lots of Fizzle Water!

But what most excited the boys' imaginations were the tins of sweet chocolate candies, like the ones Father might bring home for Mother's birthday, so dear, only one piece for each child. And here, so many!

"Hiram Mead might be a slippery snake," whispered awestruck Gideon Howe. "But he's sure got a pile of money."

"It sure seems to me," agreed his brother Tim, "that Fizzle Water selling is better than farming, or working at a mill."

But the sight of all this splendor was troubling to their brother Will.

Revelry

On Hiram Mead's fancy new parlor, beyond the long Chickering piano, the fifteen-foot fir tree was raised, with bows and beads and tinsel garland, and candles for Christmas Eve. On top, a shimmering brass angel. Underneath, an enormous pile of packages, wrapped in foil and flowered paper, tied with bright satin bows.

Five days before Christmas, the cooks arrived, a man and a woman from France. Now appeared the pastries, and cakes and breads, glazed and fruited. Sauces, for turkey and goose. Filling the air with smells to make the trespassers swoon.

And then, as they hid behind the chimney, peering in through a parlor window, she caught them in the act!

"Would you like some chocolate, William Christian? And also some for your friends?"

They were frozen in their tracks.

"Don't fret," she said. "No one will know."

When they could catch their breath, they turned to see her, the beautiful girl in satin dress and lacy shawl, extending the bright-colored shiny tin box.

"Here, William," she smiled. "You first."

Promptly, William stepped out from behind the chimney, pulled off his gray woolen mitten, and reached out a steady hand.

"Take the gold one," Victoria commanded. "It has a cherry inside."

He obeyed, reaching into the box to take his prize, peeling the foil, dropping the candy into his mouth. But scarcely had he begun to savor the smooth, sweet chocolate, the crunch of the candied fruit, its dark liquid stinging his tongue, when the harsh voice through the window made them jump.

"Victoria! What are you doing out there!"

Calmly, she turned, as William ducked back with his brothers, shivering in their hiding place.

"It is all right, Father," she called. "I am just catching a breath of fresh air."

"Well, get yourself back in here, girl! You'll catch your death!"

The window banged shut, and Victoria sighed.

"Quick!" she whispered, beckoning to the trespassers. "Hold out your hands!"

And she poured out the foil gems—red, green, silver, gold—until the bright tin box was almost empty and their cold gloved hands were filled. .

"Come back again," she whispered. "You don't need to be afraid."

But however much they enjoyed the treasure of Christmas chocolates stuffed into the pockets of their winter coats, neither Tim nor Gideon ever dared return, nor did they ever dare speak openly of their benefactress, the strange girl at Meadside Farm.

William, however, was undaunted. In the very last moment, she had delivered the ultimate treasure to him—the bright tin box itself, and all that remained within. What a risk! For surely such an object would be missed.

Certainly, he had courage enough to match hers. She had bidden him come back. And what was there to fear?

Two days before Christmas, as the fancy guests began to arrive, William Howe was eyewitness, hiding behind Rosalind O'Doule's silly new wishing well.

William had never before seen the likes of these resplendent city people, spilling from sleighs, laughing, their heads thrown back, frosty breath on the air. Their arms around each other, their smooth leather gloves clapped and stroked, fur hats tumbling to the snow, high-heeled leather boots sliding on the icy path.

Holding his breath to keep still, Will watched the scene in wonder. One of the men, holding one of the women in his arms, began to sing (in a slurring sort of voice), "*Come to me, my melancholy baa—by. Cuddle up, and donn't feel bluuuuue!*"

Another man laughed, "Melancholy baby! That's our Maudie, all right!"

Laughing, stumbling, coughing, they reached the steps, gloved hands pressing their chests. "Here we are!" they proclaimed, reaching the door. "We made it!" they laughed. "Wherever it is!" they gestured to the sky.

From the doorway, the light spilled out to the steps, down the path, to pull them in to yet more noise and laughter inside.

Sleighful after sleighful of people arrived. Beautiful, fur-clad women, with chopped-off hair, bare ankles!, sparkling jewelry, long glowing strands of beads. Handsome men with white spats, carrying long black cases and trunks.

And then music began inside, a blaring-wailing-hopping kind of music that William had never heard before. *"Come on along! Come on along! It's Alexander's Ragtime Band!"*

Spellbound, Willie stayed too long. Arms wrapped across his body, he searched each blazing window of the house. In all this time, he had caught not a single glimpse of Victoria among these noisy people!

Stamping his freezing feet, pounding fist into palm, he thought of his own warm kitchen, of his family around the hearth, his mother reading to them from one of her books, his father in his rocking chair near the fire. (How angry his father would be to know he was lurking about Hiram Mead's Fizzle Water Fortress!)

Thinking of home only made him colder. His hands and feet were numb, and the damp was reaching his bones. He drew a deep breath, and the cold air sliced his lungs. He had stayed much much too long.

With one last hopeful glance toward the bright windows, he turned away, heading out into the dark starless night, toward the forbidden short cut across the wall. He could only hope the coming storm (once more he searched the sky) would obscure his trail before morning.

Sighting on the lights from the windows at Howeside, he pressed through the hemlock hedge. Shivering from the cold, he scrambled across the wall, knocking three stones out of place.

"What's this, boy!" His father loomed from the orchard, catching him by the collar, threatening to tan his hide.

Convicted, Will remained silent.

"Don't be a darned fool, boy!" his father scowled. "A trespasser can get himself shot!"

Numb, William stumbled along the path to the house, wondering at his father's rage.

"Nothing but a bunch of loose theatricals and crooked politicians!" muttered Luther Howe, pushing his eldest son before him, trudging to his stone house in the snow.

~

The reveling begun on the twenty-third was soaring by Christmas Eve, warring in the clear night air, at least as far as Howeside, with the sound of the old church bells. Which put Luther Howe, ushering his family into the sleigh for the evening service, into a mood most foul.

"That blamed fool noise!" he complained, at the bouncy tune floating across the pond.

(Everybody's doin' it, doin' it, doin' it!)

"The Turkey Trot," smiled Hannah Howe, handing the baby to her daughter Mildred, so that two-year-old Margaret might climb into her lap.

"What are you talking about, woman!" growled her husband, lifting the lantern to light the path for his mother, coming from the house on William's arm.

"A new dance they do in the city, Luther," Hannah smiled, ignoring his mood. "Priscilla heard it in Boston, and she sang me the tune. I find it stays in the mind."

"Well, put it out of your mind!" Luther Howe commanded. "It's Christmas, darn it all!"

Climbing into the sleigh, Rebecca Howe sighed at her son's harsh words to his wife. She knew from experience that her interference would be effort spent in vain. She turned her attentions instead to her grandson, a big gentle boy with a heart that gave her hope.

"Has it been a good birthday then, William?"

"Yes, Grandmother," Will smiled. "Thank you again for the gift."

"Good things come to good boys, my child."

And as William squinted through the darkness at the bright lights beyond the hemlock trees, his grandmother settled in for the ride.

Head bent, Luther clucked to the horses, intent upon Birchwood Hill. Down the lane to Old Trail Road, across the bridge, along Church Lane, around Wooded Knoll, and up the hill. Sleigh meeting sleigh, neighbors greeting neighbors, the sounds of sleigh bells mingling, a cheerful dissonance, drowning out the last blaring trumpet, the last wailing trombone from the heathen revel at Meadside Farm.

Silent, Rebecca Howe sat as Luther guided the horses along the sleigh-slicked trail, past the coal-black wrought-iron fence enclosing the churchyard, its silent graves cloaked in fresh-fallen snow, its great elms naked against the winter sky. She sat silent as Luther reined the horses before the door of the church, for the familiar ritual, the putting down of wives and children, the men driving off to hitch the horses. And now the cheerful greetings . . . and the careful ones.

First to alight, William helped his grandmother down, hearing his Uncle Ned chiding Rufus Mead:

"What say, Rufus? Good enough to build his

house, but not quite fit for the celebration?"

Without a word, Rufus Mead steered his family away, toward the east aisle of the church, while Ned Howe turned toward the west, to follow his own family in.

He was caught in the act, however.

"Ned!" called Rebecca Howe, on the arm of her grandson Will.

At the church door Ned Howe stopped, and turned with a open arms. "Merry Christmas, Mother!" he called, greeting her with a kiss for her cheek. "Aren't you looking well! Children, look here! It's your Grandmother Howe!"

With his family—aunts and uncles and cousins— assembling at the door to the church, Young William, for the first time in his life, took this conscious thought: The west aisle. Always the same. He had never once in his life walked down the east aisle.

He watched another family approach, the Hollanders, parents and seven children, dividing at the door, some down the east aisle, others down the west, entering a center pew from either side. Not everybody has their own aisle, thought Will. Only Howes and Meads. A troubling thought, a dark spot in Will's mind, but a welcome notion all the same. For tonight he would write it in his book.

Will felt relief. It was good to have made an important observation such as this, for a certain matter had been weighing on his mind since he opened his gift from his grandmother that morning at breakfast. A leatherbound notebook with fine white pages, a new pen, and a pot of ink. To use, Grandmother had told him, in keeping with his "spiritual" gifts. For it was clear, she said, that no one in the family since the passing of his father's mother, Miriam, had possessed such a way with words.

But what did this mean? What must he do?

"Happy Birthday, William!" smiled Aunt Caroline, startling him from his thoughts.

"Twelve years old!" said Uncle Ned, clapping him on the back. "And look at the size of you already! You'll be a man, ere long."

Surrender

*T*he commotion at Meadside went on through Christmas, and continued for the next seven days, carriages coming and going, in and out of town. Even a place as grand as Mead Mansion could not house all the reveling guests. Every available spare room in town was let and let again. Every extra pound of butter and cream and sugar were summoned, every egg, every bag of flour. Every horse and sleigh were borrowed, for the coming and going, and for reveling in the snow-covered hills.

The pleasure of his Sunday dinner spoiled, Luther Howe complained: "Disturbance of the peace, is what it is! A man can't rest in his own home on the Sabbath Day!"

"My sentiments exactly, Luther," his sister-in-law Caroline sighed, hanging up the dishtowel and joining the men. "I wonder what's in that Fizzle Water anyway. Those people don't seem to need any sleep."

"Just a couple of winks between milking time and noon is all," smirked her husband, Ned.

"That is the way some city folk live," observed Rebecca, with a weary glance at her sons, and she settled into her old oak rocking chair by the fire.

"Especially artists and musicians and such," agreed Luther's wife, Hannah, shedding her apron and taking a chair beside her husband at the fire. "Priscilla says—"

But Luther Howe was fed up with unsteady "artists and musicians and such" sliding across to his side of the pond at any hour of the day or night, laughing and shouting and carrying on. Fed up, too, with silly Priscilla Brown's pretensions to city sophistication, luring his wife to idle fancies.

"Nonsense, Hannah," he growled, shifting in his chair, pulling it closer to the hearth. "They're just people, like anybody else. Only they don't do anything useful. Can't even chop their own wood!"

Rebecca watched her eldest son, his body coiled tight around emotions beyond his comprehension,

some of them partaking more of his father's unre-
solved grief, carried with him into the grave, than with
Luther's own heart.

Carefully, in the silence following Luther's implied
accusations, Rebecca picked up her knitting. There
was no sin in her grandsons, Porter and Charlie,
Elspeth's and Reah's grown sons, accepting pay (an
amount so high! never heard of before in these parts)
to replenish the woodpile at Meadside Farm. They
were young men, about to married, and the money
was a boon. No sin in this, and no betrayal. It was
about time her family remember that there was no
reason at all that a Howe couldn't work for a Mead.
Perhaps, Rebecca dared hope, this monstrosity Hiram
had created could somehow, in spite of itself—

A sudden "BOOM" from the direction of the
pond, accompanied by a chorus of joyous shrieking,
brought Luther to his feet.

"I'd like to get out my horsewhip," he bellowed,
"and teach those *city folk* some manners."

"You'd do better to attend to the beam in your
own eye, Luther," warned Rebecca, with a sharp
glance toward her son. And then, laying aside her
knitting and summoning her grandson William, she
gestured toward the thick black volume on the window table. "Fetch me the Good Book, my son. I'd like
to read."

~

At last it was time for the grand hurrah, with fire-works (and fist-fights) exploding, to welcome in the New Year.

"Nothing but a drunken brawl over there, no matter how fancy they think they are," Luther grumbled, pulling his nosy boys (yet again) back from the wall. "Nothing but devilment and waste."

Soon enough, the revelers were leaving, drooping, quiet, blinking as if the afternoon light were painful, sharp on new-fallen snow.

("That Fizzle Water's got some mighty peculiar effects all right.")

And then, they were gone.

But not before Will Howe, risking the journey one last time, saw and heard what broke his heart: Hiram Mead in a terrible rage, and Rosalind O'Doule, as well.

At the end of the walk, the sleigh stood ready, loaded with trunks and leather cases. While, on the littered porch Victoria stood in her red-velvet cape, silent, alone, a small brown valise at her feet.

In and out of the house, her parents carried on, both of them hurling dishes, curses, accusations, flinging luggage, clothing, bottles, even food!

"Victoria," he whispered, stepping forward as her parents retreated once more into the house.

"Hello, William," she said quite calmly. "Did you have a nice Christmas?"

He opened his mouth to speak—

"And happy birthday, by the way," she remarked. (But she was not looking at him.)

"I . . . I just came over to say—"

The front door flew suddenly open, and out burst Rosalind O'Doule, sailing across the porch and down the icy steps, steady on her feet.

Frozen to the spot, Will watched in amazement, as Rosalind marched down the front path. (She didn't seem to notice him at all.)

Where is she going? he wondered, watching her pass the sleigh and march out into the lane. She isn't even wearing a coat!

From the porch, Victoria examined the sky.

"Take it! Take it all!" Hiram Mead shouted from the house.

On the porch, Victoria sighed.

And now he appeared in the doorway, shouting after his wife. "Here!" He flung something shiny in her direction. "You certainly deserve every cent!"

Hiram's aim was wide of his mark, and a shower of silver fell instead at William's feet, the coins pelting deep into the snow.

"Easy come, easy go," Will heard Rosalind remark, with a toss of flaming red curls.

And now came Hiram in black overcoat. Eyes forward, he pointed to the sleigh.

Thus commanded, Victoria followed.

Invisible in plain sight in the yard at Meadside Farm (a handful of silver dollars at his feet), William Howe watched them go, Victoria and her father in the sleigh, retrieving Rosalind from the lane, and then streaking down Old Trail Road, the horses whipped into a lather, off to meet the Boston train.

("Good riddance!" was the quick consensus of the Bell Falls Ladies' League.)

This was the beginning, and the end, of Hiram Mead's Glorious Country Retreat in Old Bell Falls. No idle weekends, no languid summers, no more winter revels. The house stood closed, weathering in silence, extravagant furnishings bedraggled with the artifacts of one startling, splendorous Christmas.

Once more, silence reigned on Meadside. Year after year, the grounds lay untended, the barn and carriage house empty, but for the mice and the bats. Nobody went near. No one made any claims.

"He'll be back, you can bet on it," a Mead, from time to time, would be heard to promise.

"There's a curse on the place, mark my words," would warn any Howe you might meet. And the children whispered of ghosts.

Times changed. The country entered the War-to-End-All-Wars. A Mead and two Howes gave their lives, mourned by relations on opposite aisles of the church, divided, even in grief.

The war, no doubt, was the reason for Cousin Hiram's absence, George and Rufus Mead decided. After the war, he would turn up. (Like a bad penny, groused Luther Howe.) And things would crank up at Meadside once again.

After a time, however, rumors floated over from Boston. Concerning Rosalind O'Doule running off to

South America with an acrobatic Russian Count. Concerning Hiram, broke and in trouble up to his neck, driving off the pier into Boston Harbor in yet another brand spanking new motorcar.

Leaving Victoria . . . she would be sixteen years old now or thereabouts . . . leaving Victoria, where?

No one wondered about Victoria Mead more often than William Howe, his tin box (lined with a dozen silver coins he was saving for her) filling with words.

Each year on his birthday his grandmother gave him another leatherbound notebook, and a pot of ink, and a new set of pens. By the end of each year, the book would be dutifully filled and laid in the shiny box.

On Armistice Day in 1918, Rebecca Howe, failing from congestion in the lungs, requested that she be moved from her daughter Elspeth's house in town out to the old homestead at Howeside, to pass her last days in sight of Abnak Pond, sheltered under the roof her Ephraim had raised.

It was here, wrapped in patchwork in her oak rocking chair by the fire, that Rebecca breathed her last.

"Fetch me the Good Book, William," she whispered, raising a feeble hand. "I'd like to read."

Will knelt at her side, the Bible in his hands, "Remember, my son," she whispered, her last words. "Remember you have come to bring peace."

On the following Christmas Eve, his eighteenth birthday, William Christian Howe wrote the last words in his last leather book. Closing the cover upon the words, he laid the volume with the others, in Victoria Mead's shiny tin box. A tight fit, for the box was full (a dozen silver dollars its foundation). He must tie the lid on with string.

Time now to put the box away. To put away his childhood thoughts, the record he had made of his family, under his grandmother's charge: what he had observed, what he had guessed, what he had felt. But it was time to put away the words of a boy, and enter the world of men.

Speculation

Villiam Christian Howe, as his father intended, took up the carpenter's trade, until his skill at woodworking was known for a hundred miles around.

In his twenty-third year, he was married to Miss Abigail Waite of Littleton, New Hampshire, whose father, Mr. Theodore Waite, Esq., had commissioned an entire dining room for his wife, Lydia.

Watching the young craftsman unload his excellent work from the wagon (carrying the entire table on his back!) Miss Abigail had been smitten. But hearing him express keen interest in the philosophies of Mr.

Emerson and Mr. Thoreau, she was captured, more than willing to live out her days in remote little Old Bell Falls.

The new Mr. and Mrs. Howe set up housekeeping at Howeside Farm, so that when William's mother Hannah was gone, they assumed the care of his father Luther, who had been disabled by stroke.

Presently, I, James William Howe, am born, followed by Jacob, Susannah, Andrew, Daniel, Octavia, and Tess. We were blessed to inhabit a generations–old farm, in a quaint village nestled in a green mountain valley, a picturesque Christmas-card place, spiced with (even more important for our childish imaginations) an elegant (perhaps even haunted!) eyesore on the other side of the pond.

We drew security from the fact that Bell Falls was home to a goodly number of our relations—farmers, sawyers, craftsmen, and even a preacher (Uncle Gideon)—whose mutual avocations consisted of arguing over the elegant eyesore and carefully tending a wall to keep nobody out.

"We ought to buy them out and knock the place down," thought Great-uncle Ned. "Put the land back into pasture."

"A shame to waste a good large building," thought my father. "The construction is sound—"

"Well, no one is going to live there," said Uncle

Tim. "Who could afford these days to keep up a place that size?"

"I heard that one of George Mead's boys is thinking of turning it into a hotel," worried Great-uncle Isaac.

"Heaven forbid!" prayed Uncle Gideon.

"I believe I hear Old Ephraim turning in his grave," winked Great-uncle Ned.

My mother, small, refined in the midst of these substantial, rugged Howes, merely rolled her eyes.

It was the picturesque, no doubt, that brought them back—Hiram's daughter, Victoria, with her husband, Stuart Stethington, the supposedly famous landscape painter that nobody had ever heard of, and the ten-year-old boy, Gamaliel Stethington-Mead.

We caught our first glimpse of him the very first day. Skinny, awkward, close curly hair the color of a dusty lamb, he was struggling to pull an over-sized painting easel from the back of the green Touring Car.

"That," said my brother Jacob, "is the dumbest looking kid I ever seen."

"Saw," I corrected.

"Meads is just stupid is all," said Jake.

"Are stupid," I corrected.

"Think for yourself, boys," said Father, joining us at the wall. "Don't just repeat what you've heard."

Up at the house, Aunts Margaret and Mildred and Faith and Iris had come to finish Cousin Naomi's wedding quilt. "Gamaliel," sniffed Aunt Mildred, taking a perfect stitch.

"What kind of a name is that?" sniffed Aunt Meg, bending over to check my mother's work for perfection.

"It's in the Bible, I think," observed my mother, bringing a needle up under Margaret's nose.

Aunt Iris clasped her hands beneath her generous bosom and assumed her Sunday School air: "The Book of Acts. The teacher of the Apostle Paul."

"You mean, he was a Jew?" Aunt Faith was a trifle confused.

"Who?" wondered Aunt Millie.

"The Apostle Paul."

"I thought you meant Gamaliel."

"The Meads have never been Jewish, Mildred!"

"What are you talking about, Faith?"

"I suppose it just sounds better that way," Mother mused, ignoring the lot of them. "Mead-Stethington wouldn't be nearly as . . . *euphonious* as Stethington-Mead."

"Euphonious, smonious, Abigail," Aunt Meg insisted. "A name like that is suspicious."

Aunt Mildred could not agree more. "Suspicious, and not altogether proper."

Proper, Victoria Mead (Stethington) was not. All through the valley, people talked. In the farmhouses, in the shops, in the schoolyard, even in church. Where had she been? What had she known? What could be read in that expressionless face, in the delicate, china-white features, drawn slightly, as if waiting for breath.

As for the elegance, it could be an act. (Her red-haired mother, after all, had been a *theatrical* person.) The clothing was very fine, to be sure. Expensive perhaps, but not new.

If they had money to spend, Mr. & Mrs. Stethington (Mead), they went to no great expense to fix up Meadside Farm. They hired a couple of girls from town to shovel out nearly twenty years of corruption and make the house fit for habitation. They commandeered a couple of strapping young fellows from the coal yard to clear weeds and cut a path to the door.

But mostly, Stuart Stethington seemed to want the place as it was, natural and wild, to please his artist's eye.

And what did *she* do while the artist, from a dozen perspectives, scrutinized the house, the outbuildings, and the long row of fifty-year-old hemlocks along the quaint rock wall?

What did *she* do while he tromped through the countryside in silk scarf and black wool beret, setting up easels, mixing up paints, wielding brushes, painting landscapes of the fields, the meadows, and the pond?

What did *she* do while he waltzed about town, nodding to the townsfolk, as if they were on display?

What did she do, then, while he courted the picturesque?

She played on the old grand piano in the parlor, which somehow she had tuned by herself. Or she unpacked her books, boxes and boxes of books, reading as she went, not upright in a proper chair, but stretched, languid, upon the fainting couch, her pale limbs draped in gauze. Reading and reading at all hours of the day and night, until you'd have thought she might go blind.   And what did she read?

Not almanacs or catalogues or cookbooks or other useful tomes, but disreputable volumes on exotic travel, foreign religions, modern philosophy. Fictitious novels, too.   Jane Austen, Nathaniel Hawthorne, and Henry James.

The highly esteemed Bell Falls Ladies' Welcoming Committee, delivering the basket of homemade bread and home-bottled jam, saw these things with their very own eyes.

While we, my cousins and brothers and I, saw through the sheer parlor curtains the curly-haired boy in the sailor suit, playing with his mechanical toys, or curling up beside his beautiful mother, his head in her lap as she read to him, stroking his hair.

We would never admit it to one another, but we were envious from the first, peering through the windows at the painted tin wonders: windup clowns, friction cars, a steam engine that ran on kerosene and raised a tiny tin bucket on pulleys; armies of tin soldiers, infantry, and cavalry on tin horses.

We watched, bolder and bolder, as they seemed to take no notice of us at all—he with his wondrous toys, and she in pale satin and gauze, her china-white brow furrowed in concentration, poring over her books.

Until, called home for evening chores, we would tear ourselves away from the enchantments of the idle.

Back in the real world of hard work, we watched our mother, fresh from a meeting of the Ladies' League (where the known world was . . . not *judged*, for that would be sin . . . but evaluated with great care) ladle soup into the supper bowls with vigor.

"I don't mean to criticize your family again, William. But I have never in my life known such a collection of prejudicial, narrow-minded gossips."

"I'd say that was a fair enough evaluation, Abby," my father smiled.

"I wonder what those people eat over there in that big old house?" she murmured, reaching for my father's bowl. "Not that I'm being nosy myself . . ."

"Why don't you go over and find out, my love?" said my father, savoring the aroma of soup.

"That would be all right with you?" She looked at him with mild surprise.

"Why ever not?"

"Mildred said . . . " She paused, taking her place at the table.

"What did Mildred say?"

"She said you knew her as a child."

"Victoria, you mean. I met her, spoke to her once or twice. She was a lovely, lonely child." He hesitated, thinking. "She gave us, my brothers and me, some candy once, the year they were out for Christmas."

"And?"

"And what?"

"Mildred said—"

"The less you listen to my sisters, dear Abigail, the better off you'll be."

"They can't last long over there in that big cold house," said Mother, slicing the bread.

"There was the box, of course," said Father, musing once again. "After she gave us the candy, she gave me the empty box. It was generous, it seemed to me. And brave." He looked around the table at six waiting faces. "I put my childhood journals in it. I found they fit just right."

My mother sighed, and passed the bread. "They

will be gone before winter comes," she said. "Unless I miss my guess."

"I expect you're right," said Father, folding his strong rough hands and turning to me. "James, you will please bless our food."

It was a quiet meal, unusual at our table.

Until, finished with his apple pie, Father pulled off his napkin and pushed back his chair. "Abigail," he said, standing up. "I have something that belongs to Victoria Mead. It's time we made our call."

"I wondered when we would," said Mother, mild as milk.

Gamaliel

They took their time, Father and Mother, walking over from Howeside together, hand in hand. We spied on them through the hemlocks, from our favorite crumbly spot along the wall, where a few missing stones made space for a comfortable perch. I had brought out my Sears-Roebuck periscope, to get a better view.

It was Gamaliel, his knickerbocker pants buttoned just below the knee, who opened the door. (Later, our mother would repeat to us his exact words, as if they should be an example to us all.)

"Good day, Mr. and Mrs. Howe. It is nice of you

to come. We regret that we are unable to receive visitors at this time. Thank you very much for your trouble."

And, solemnly accepting the offering of fresh harvest bread and blueberry jam (and, unknowingly, of a dozen silver coins slipped into the bottom of the basket), he silently closed the door.

Our parents did not, I think, turn back to see. But I saw, through my scope, Victoria Mead at a third-story window, curtain pulled back, watching them depart.

Against all predictions, they stayed, on through the end of summer and into autumn, taking tours through the hills in their wonderful Touring Car—the painter smiling and waving to the colorful locals; the lovely Victoria pale, impassive, gazing forward, neither extending nor accepting a greeting of any sort, always with the same fine mask; the boy Gamaliel beside her, stock still, as if managing fear.

My parents never tried to visit them again, as far as I knew, and no one else seemed interested in making the effort.

"Some folks, I guess, are just plain unsociable," declared Aunt Meg.

While Aunt Mildred was of sterner opinion: "Some folks just have too much to hide."

From time to time the hired girls came out to cook and clean, taking back news to fuel "evaluations."

News of Stuart Stethington's bizarre, unseemly behavior, of Victoria's odd persistent silence. And, most alarmingly, news of a boy ten years old without normal associations, who spent hours upon end with his head in his mother's lap, and who probably could not even read!

Aunt Mildred and Aunt Meg, in consultation with Aunt Iris and Aunt Faith, thought that Uncle Tim, now constable and unofficial truant officer, might take some sort of legal action.

But Uncle Tim (perhaps under the memory of a sweet-faced girl and a bounteous gift of shimmering foil-wrapped chocolate) seemed to lack sufficient aggression.

"Just keep in mind," Tim chuckled to his fretting female relations, "what the Good Book says about minding our own business."

But even Uncle Pastor Gideon's wife, the Excellent Aunt Iris, hadn't heard that one before.

At any rate, in the midst of all the fretting, the boy, one day without warning, showed up at the old red schoolhouse on his own.

He stood there hugging a worn leather satchel at the gate. Gamaliel Stethington-Mead, in white shirt, blue bow tie, and those silly knickerbocker pants.

At any rate, in the midst of all the fretting, the boy, one day without warning, showed up at the old red schoolhouse on his own.

He stood there hugging a worn leather satchel at the gate. Gamaliel Stethington-Mead, in white shirt, blue bow tie, and those silly knickerbocker pants.

Rugged in our denim overalls and thick wool trousers, chafing in our Sears-Roebuck shirts, we jeered him, opened the gate, drew him in, the better to torment him, scuffing our boots at him, jostling him in the yard. Merciless, we teased him with frogs and snakes, slimy rodents, and bugs.

Silent, he turned from us, clutching his books.

"C'mon, Gamey!" we taunted. "Don't you want to play!"

"Be a sport, Gamayleeul!" we shouted, forming our crack-the-whip line. "Come on! You'll like this, you'll see!"

"Gamey, mamey, what a shamey!" shouted my second cousin Nate, making a dash for Gamaliel and grabbing him by the arm. His books went flying, but he made no protest as Nate pulled him to the end of the line.

Slowly through the schoolyard, we began to snake, Gamaliel held fast at the tail of the whip. Faster and faster we pulled him, around in a figure-eight, until, at the right moment, Nate let go, sending Gamaliel flying across the yard.

Safe (and innocent) in the middle of the line, I watched him land in the dust, skidding on his knees, ripping his corduroy pants.

Holding my breath, I watched Gamaliel, while the others ran away. He touched his head with a bloody hand, blood, too, at his elbows and knees. In the very next moment, I would have gone to his rescue, I was sure. But, in a flash, Miss Cowdery had reached him, was helping him rise, coughing, to his feet.

All the way to the schoolhouse he limped, blood streaking down his bare legs and into his high-topped shoes. He held his head as he coughed, wheezing from the dust. I watched him disappear with Miss Cowdery into the schoolhouse, the heavy door banging shut.

Alone under the old maple tree, holding on to the rope swing for support, I felt my heart go tight. Not only had I betrayed Gamaliel, but also, somehow, I had let my father down.

"It was an accident, Father," I told him, my face burning from the lie. "He isn't used to our rough play."

"Yeah," confirmed my brother Andy. "Nate was just invitin' him. Nobody meant no harm."

My father looked away from us, jaw working, eyes squinting, gazing out through the kitchen window in the direction of Meadside Farm, while Mother occupied herself with the correcting of Andrew's grammar.

And so the subject of Gamaliel Stethington-Mead's reception at Bell Falls School was officially dropped.

I heard them discussing it, though, Father and Mother, late at night.

Mother had come in from gathering the windfall apples, carrying a basket full of wildflowers. The very basket she had given to Victoria Mead.

"I found it on the wall, William," she told my father, lifting her eyes (which from the sound of her voice must have been filled with tears).

"It's a beautiful gift, Abby," my father agreed.

"As long as I live I will never understand your family, William," she said, arranging the flowers in a vase. "What is the matter with you Howes and Meads?"

"I wish I could say, Abigail," my father sighed.

My mother took Victoria's gesture as an opening, but, in fact, it seemed it was not. If anything, peculiar Hiram Mead's peculiar daughter became ever more remote, more reserved, more inaccessible. My mother's hopes for a companion in Old Bell Falls, someone to share her lofty thoughts, her yearnings for culture, were dashed. (Which hopes were now turned with new vigor upon my sisters, and me.)

As for Gamaliel, his tenure in fifth grade was begun and concluded on a single October morning, after which he was again at home every day, leaving only for walks to the pond, where the geese seemed tame at his call, or to venture out into the hills with the painter, who scouted the old Indian trails, as if sporting a fondness for manly adventure.

Distant witness to Gamaliel's autumn idyll, I let my guilt fade away. Wasn't Gamaliel, after all, the freest, luckiest boy in town?

Except that, even I, a mere child, could detect something odd, something slightly amiss in Stuart Stethington—a restlessness about the eyes, a falter in the bravado, and even, from time to time, a certain cruelty in the smile.

Finally, as the days grew shorter, Gamaliel merely watched while the artist did nothing but paint the pond, trying, it seemed, to perfectly reproduce the effect of water in every light: *"The Pond at Dawn."*

"Morning Sunlight on the Pond." "The Pond in Autumn, at Noonday." "Sunset Over Abnak Pond."

"Dull," we heard the painter sigh, as we spied on him from beyond the wall. "Too, too deadly dull."

What does a painter want at the pond in the dark? I wondered. For we saw him, bareheaded, alone under the Indian Summer moon, listening, it seemed, to the nothing of night.

At last we became aware that he was gone. The green Touring Car was still hidden away in the carriage house, but for several days running we had seen Gamaliel alone, staring across the pond, downriver, toward the falls.

"Maybe he ran out of paint," said Mother, in that bland way of hers that always made Father smile. And then, "Perhaps she will leave now as well."

She did not leave, however. She did not leave at all. Never even left the house. The two hired girls did the shopping for food, while Victoria drifted about the rooms all day, dressed in a filmy gown, wrapped in a knotted shawl, playing her piano, or reading her books in the parlor with sad red eyes.

"How can she possibly stay out there all winter?" wondered Aunt Meg, at work among the ruins of the Thanksgiving feast. "Without a man about the place."

"You would call that painter of hers a *man*?" sniffed Aunt Mildred, delivering table scraps into the slop-bucket by the kitchen door.

"I have heard that she reads those modern paper-covered novels," deplored Aunt Iris, guarding her heart with her hand.

"What use has a woman for all this study, whatever she reads!" declared Aunt Faith, polishing dinner plates.

"Indeed," intoned The Reverend Uncle Gideon, "the Holy Bible itself cautions moderation, and is of itself enough. Faith, after all, is a simple thing."

"She sure is," chuckled Uncle Tim, looking up from his newspaper to give his wife a wink.

Aunt Faith was not amused. "The woman is not reliable, and the child is not cared for properly!"

"Well, she did try to send him to school," sighed my father, eyeing my brothers and cousins and me.

"And she does read from the Bible," said my mother, also with an eye to us boys. "Surely you all have heard the rumors to that effect." Wiping her hands on her apron, she handed my father a stack of dishes to carry to the shelf. "How can you fret over someone who reads the Bible?"

"She rocks it, too," said my cousin Joe.

I wanted to grab him and stifle him good.

"What do you mean, Joseph?" asked Aunt Faith, seizing him by the arm.

"She rocks it, Mother," he said, wrenching away.

"Croons to it, like it was a baby."

"I think she's just praying is all," said my brother Jake, just as dumb as Joe.

"If she wants to pray, she should be in Church!" declared Aunt Iris, with a meaningful nod toward Husband Gideon, who beamed back approval upon her.

Seeing as how Joe and Jake had tipped our hand, we boys moved together, edging toward the stairs to the loft.

Father, however, intervened, looming over us, spreading his massive arms, like the veritable shadow of God. "Have you boys been spying on Meadside Farm again, or just listening to the idle gossip of your elders?"

We shrank, slipping away up the stairs.

"She will be gone by Christmas, mark my words," I heard Aunt Iris declare.

"For an gentler, easier life elsewhere, would be our fervent wish," insisted The Reverend Uncle Gideon at her side.

From the rocking chair by the fire, came the familiar moan. Grandfather Luther, as if in pain, yet no pain on his impassive face.

My father turned, moving toward the still form in the chair.

"Come, Gideon," he beckoned to his youngest

brother. "Our father is tired. Help me put Old Luther to bed."

~

Throughout the splendid autumn, Gamaliel was free. We saw him as we trudged, too soon forced into winter woollies, sweating and itching, to and from the stuffy old red schoolhouse. We saw him staring out over the freezing pond, skipping rocks, hearing birds, watching the Canadian geese come down in perfect formation, honking their way to warmer climes.

While we slogged in the mud to feed the stock, milk the cows, tend the horses, split logs for the winter fires, bring in the pumpkins, mend the fences, repair the wall, we saw through our frosty breath the form on the other side of the pond, drinking in autumn. Idle.

The womenfolk could not conquer their alarm.

"That boy should be usefully occupied," Aunt Mildred insisted, examining the log-cabin pattern of the new quilt-top for flaws.

"Idle hands are the devil's workshop," agreed Aunt Iris, pulling a sturdy two-foot-long cotton thread through the heavy batting.

"He will be a burden on the community one day," prophesied Aunt Faith, the silver thimble gleaming upon the tip of her upraised index finger.

"He is ill," explained my mother, surrendering her needle and thread to Aunt Meg. "There is something wrong with his lungs."

"He should not be spending all day in the out of doors, then," warned Aunt Meg, deftly poking the thread through the slender eye of the needle and returning it to my mother. "He will catch his death!"

And then, busy around the quilt they would forthwith donate to charity, they started in about how long the woodpile at Meadside might last, about doctors, and "What Any Decent Mother Would Do in Such a Situation."

"She has a shelf full of books about poisons!" Aunt Faith had heard.

"Herbal remedies, rather," thought my mother.

"Her pantry," intoned Aunt Mildred, "is filled with—"

"Evil-smelling concoctions!" triumphed Meg.

"Perhaps the evil is in the mind of the beholder, Margaret," remarked my father, making an unexpected intrusion from the kitchen.

"Watch your muddy boots, William," retorted his sister. "You will spoil Abigail's clean floor."

Mischief

*N*ow, the end of my story begins on a chilly Saturday afternoon between Thanksgiving and Christmas, a clear day after a good hard snow.

A gang of us—my two brothers and sister and I, quite a number of our first-cousins, second-cousins, and sundry cousins-once-removed—were down at the pond, testing the ice.

Daring one another, we edged out, braving the creaking, defying the terrifying BOOM! as the deep cracks moved far beneath us, out toward the falls.

Satisfied that the ice was not yet ready for sliding or skating, we huddled together on the bank, trying to start a fire with kindling we hauled out on a sled.

Shivering, we waited while cousins Henry and Nate worked to strike a spark. At last, the damp logs caught, and we moved back from the smoke.

"Bring over the seats!" commanded Henry, and each of us found his own—a rock, a crate, a stump of wood. I found an old rusty tractor seat for my sister Susannah, while Henry and Nate claimed the sled.

As the afternoon shadows lengthened over the glazing surface of Abnak Pond, we sat there thus crudely enthroned, in a ring around the smoky fire, snow melting into puddles at our feet.

In a moment, Henry leaned forward, a look of mischief in his eyes. "She's here, you know," Henry whispered, sending shivers down my spine.

"Who?" shuddered Susannah, who had begged to come out with the boys.

"The ghost of Marguerite LaPointe!"

"Aw, go on," scoffed Cousin Nate.

But now Henry stood, creeping back toward the edge of the pond, hunched over like a ghoul.

"She's here, I tell you," he whispered. "Can't you hear her?"

The cold wind was rising, picking up drifted snow, rustling bare branches in the grove of ghost-white birch.

"Hear it?" cried Henry, gesturing toward the falls.

"Moaning and crying, from the depths of her watery grave!"

At the fire, the little ones began to whimper.

"Stop it, Henry," I said.

But Henry was in full burn: "She's coming!" he cried. "Coming for her revenge!" And he turned, dark eyes glowing upon us, with a scream that sent the little ones shrieking up the bank.

"Who's coming?" said a calm voice behind me, the form materializing suddenly in our smoky ring.

Now the rest of us jumped, and all of us screamed. (Even Henry, though he would fiercely deny it.)

The ghostly figure was still, flanked by fleeing Howes, left and right.

At the fire, only the bravest remained, as the figure spoke again.

"Marguerite LaPointe. Who is she?" asked Gamaliel Stethington-Mead.

He stood not two feet from me, wreathed in smoke from the fire, ears red, white face puzzled under his city-boy's soft cap, not budging an inch, as Cousin Henry moved up from the bank.

"Tell me who she is," said Gamaliel again, as if unaware of Henry's rage.

I knew that Henry would never forgive this stranger, for stealing his show, for scaring him, and above all, for being a Mead. I knew I should stop this nonsense now, before it was too late. But Cousin Henry was fourteen years old, and big for his age. I was not quite twelve, and small.

Now Henry moved close to the intruder, motioning to his brother Nate, and to Cousin Pete. As the three of them circled 'round Gamaliel, Henry began to weave a fantastic tale, the likes of which I had never heard before.

"Okay, Mr. Nosy-Face," Henry sneered. "You asked, and so we'll answer."

"Yeah," said Nate, trying for menace.

"Yeah," echoed Peter at his side.

"She was a witch, if you want to know!" said Henry, pausing to lift a fist right up under Gamaliel's chin. "The beautiful witch who started it all. Between us Howes and you puny Meads."

For some reason, Gamaliel looked to me for an explanation. But I could only shrug, moving back closer to the fire, while Peter took the line:

"We hate each other, in case you didn't know it, Gamaylee-ul Stuffingtown Mead."

"And it will never change," growled Nate. "So you better go back where you came from, wherever it was."

Then Henry began to taunt, "You're cursed, you are, Gamey-mamey!" his wool-gloved hands held up like claws, "because old Nathaniel Mead murdered Ephraim Howe's girl, not far from this very spot!"

The three of them circled him, one following another in the tale, as if it were rehearsed:

"She was a witch, was Marguerite LaPointe!"

"Possessed of the devil!"

"She could capture men's souls with a glance!"

Then, in a heartbeat, the tale took a terrifying twist.

"And so is your mother, Gamey-lamey!"

"A witch!"

"Possessed by the very same devil—"

"—that took Marguerite LaPointe—"

"—to the deep, dark, slimy bottom of Abnak Pond—"

"—on Christmas Eve, long, long ago."

And then they stopped. Gamaliel closed his eyes.

Suddenly, Nate was seized with another hideous inspiration: "Ask him where his father is, Pete!"

I gasped at the cruelty of it.

And there was more.

"Better still," thought Henry, not to be outdone, "ask him *who* his father is!"

Together, my cousins laughed, terrible mocking laughter, throwing back their heads like fools.

"Maybe . . ." And Henry was the ghoul again, hunching up close, his clenched fist in Gamaliel's face. "Maybe his father is . . . the devil!"

"Stop it," I gasped in horror. And then louder,

"Stop right now!"

Gamaliel opened his eyes, and stood staring, not blinking, just working his fists, his bare ears freezing white, as Peter and Henry and Nate circled 'round him once more, teasing his chapped red cheeks with their frozen gloves:

"All of you will die, Gamey-lamey! Every one of you Meads who dares come back to Abnak Pond!"

"Stop it! Stop it!" I cried, scrambling up the bank, tugging on Henry's coat.

But Henry shrugged me off, shoving me back down the slope. Gamaliel meanwhile was moving fast, so fast I didn't see where he found the stone that struck Henry's head and spread a blood-blotch on the snow.

And just as fast, Gamaliel was gone.

Cousin Henry told Aunt Caroline and Uncle Ned, as well as Doc McDougal, who sewed up the wound, that he had slipped and fallen on the ice, cutting his head on a twig. That way, no one was suspicious. No one kept an eye out for retribution.

So there was no mercy after that, no end to the taunting, the pranks.

I watched, helpless, as my cousins grew braver, pitched dead birds and rotten apples in through broken windows at Meadside Farm, tossed frozen egg-bombs onto the porches.

They were careful. No one knew. No one stopped them. My father would have put an end to it, if I had told. But I was afraid. I had a dozen teenaged cousins—distant and near—who lived in Old Bell Falls. And a traitor to his kin was the worst thing a boy could ever be.

I made my sister stay home, and my little brothers, too. They were scared anyway, and they didn't mind. But I went along on those dark-night pranks, because I knew that I had to go.

I always told Father that I was meeting Nate and Henry and Peter, and that much wasn't a lie. He asked what we were up to, and I said we were drilling another fishing hole, or we were watching Henry tool his new saddle, or looking at the mink Nate had trapped. Those were the lies.

The last time, I said Peter had found a nest of frozen baby owls. I almost didn't get away with that one. But somehow Father let me go, even overran Mother's objections.

"You'll freeze to death one of these evenings, James," she warned.

"No need to fret, Abby. He's a country boy. And he's growing up."

"There is plenty of time to grow up in the daylight, William. Even in the country."

But, for some reason, she let me go anyway.

I hurried with chores and got away just after dark to meet the boys at the bridge below the falls. By light of the moon behind a shifting cover of clouds, we made our way around the pond and up to the Mead side of the wall, slipping into the hemlock hedge.

Across the wide expanse of untrammeled snow, the huge dark house took no heed. No sound, no movement. No one at the window, no one opening a door. Not even a single light.

"Maybe they've gone away," I hoped.

"Naw," scoffed Henry. "They're just hiding out in there."

Henry motioned that we should follow, out onto the expanse of snow. Slowly, we approached, then bolder and bolder, tramping a path in the snow. Ten of us, beginning the circle, tramping a path around the house in the snow.

And then, Henry began the chant:

Better run and hide your head,
Marg'rite LaPointe's come back from the dead!
Bother, bother, where's your father!
Ask Demon Rum! You don't have one!

Only a whisper at first, the chanting grew louder and louder, the others joining in as they learned, until anyone could have heard . . . .

I couldn't say the words, and finally I broke from the circle, catching up with Henry in the line.

"This is stupid," I whispered hoarsely. "We're going to get caught."

Henry turned on me, fierce. "You gotta decide, Jamey boy. Are you a real Howe, or not?"

He gave me a shove that sent me sprawling. On my back in the snow, I looked up at the huge dark house. It was then that I saw the light! First just a flicker in the parlor window, as if a candle or lamp had been lit deep inside the house.

Heart thudding, I scrambled to my feet, catching up with Nate, to give a tug on his coat.

"Look!" I whispered. But the light had gone out.

I saw it next on the second floor, an eerie glow, floating from room to room. But, this time, Peter saw it, too.

"Shh!" Pete whispered, silencing the chant. "What's that up there!"

"What are you talking about?"shrugged Henry, annoyed.

"Someone's watching us!"

"Where!?" Nate checked over both shoulders.

"There! In the window—!!"

The light, however, had again disappeared. And, disgusted, Henry gave Pete a punch on the shoulder. "What's the matter with you ninnies!"

But no one any longer paid Henry any mind. For they all saw it now, the strange blue light, floating through the rooms of the third floor.

"I told you we'd get caught," I tried. "You and your silly prank has woke her up—"

"No!" whispered Nate. "That's not Victoria!"

"I don't think it's even a *person*," Peter agreed. "Look how it floats!"

"Aw—" Henry began, peering toward the upper windows of the house. "Don't be stupid." But the confidence was draining from his voice.

The glow was moving again, vanishing from the third story and moving into the attic.

"I don't like this," whispered Peter.

"Me neither . . . let's get out of here . . . " The nervous murmuring was spreading through the group.

"You're all a bunch of lily-livered—!!" Henry tried. But his eyes were yet fixed upon the house.

The light now flooded the attic window, a blue figure taking shape in the glow, as all around us eerie wind-sounds rose.

I shuddered, and felt Nate shudder at my side: "It *isn't* a person!" he insisted, hoarse.

"Of course it is," demanded Henry. "What else—"

"I mean it! No *body* glows like that!"

"Cowards," Henry hissed.

"It's nothing—" I tried to believe.

~ 122 ~

But at the sight of the hazy blue-white form taking shape in the high attic window, I was not so sure myself that this was someone of this earth.

I could sense the fear around me, as I stood, shaking in my boots.

The clouds were scurrying, thicker now, the winter wind whistling through the fields, rattling the loose shutters of the house, creaking the boards of the old barn, letting loose the crows, banging open the big door of the carriage house, releasing the bats in a storm over our heads.

Suddenly, Peter was certain: "It's a ghost!" His voice was squeaky. "The ghost of . . .

"Marguerite LaPointe!" shrieked a chorus of terrified Howes.

And then, all around me, cousins were moving, backwards in the snow, stumbling over one another, a hasty retreat that even Henry's scorn could not deter.

"Cowards!" he tried again.

But we were running, taking cover behind a rusting hay wagon in the yard, watching the upstairs window, where she stood unmoving, no sign of a candle or lamp, just a whole glowing being, as if the light came from inside her. I felt regarded, exposed, as though I and I alone were the object of her gaze.

"It's like she can see us!" Peter whispered. "Even in the dark!"

"C'mon," I begged. "Let's get out of here!"

"You're such a bunch of cowards—" Henry tried once more.

But at the BANG of the screen door blowing hard against the house, he was running for Howeside beside me, all the same.

"She's coming after us!" shouted Nate, and the others began to scream, running hard, without looking back.

Reunion

*O*n the commons at the end of Main Street opposite The Sophronia Wheelwright Mead Library and Cultural Center, the hundred-fifty-year-old spruce is hung with carved figurines, and candles for Christmas Eve. Each evening, carolers grace the town-hall steps. And, under the direction of Mrs. Pastor Gideon Howe (née Iris Ann Willoughby of Brattleboro), the Ladies' League work tirelessly to prepare baskets of food for the needy.

Not many needy, of course, in these self-reliant parts. Only old Sam Wills, stubborn in his cabin, too old to properly care for himself. And Heber Jones's widow, though her sons were coming along now and will very soon take up the slack.

But in the Ladies'-League Hall (once Sophronia Mead's Grand Parlor), a days-old debate about the poor-in-spirit on the other side of Abnak Pond.

At last, a generous decision is taken: to consider her a widow, wherever the strange landscape painter had gone, whatever her just deserts, out there aloof, alone by choice, spurning all Christian kindness.

A basket, then, for the Widow Stethington-Mead. A basket, a gesture of charity, no matter how fruitless. Of charity, and good will.

"Who do they think they are, judging her like that!" I heard my father mutter. "Sitting there in her own grandmother's house like a pack of—"

But I wasn't meant to hear it, and he didn't seem to be lifting a hand himself to help her. Nor did Constable Uncle Tim. Nor more did Uncle Gideon, the man of the cloth.

It crossed my eleven-year-old mind (absolutely sure now that there had been no ghost) that Victoria Mead just needed someone smart to talk to, someone as smart as she was. But I couldn't think who that would be (except for perhaps my mother).

The Howe boys, their minds on Christmas (and wary of Meadside Farm), abandoned their pranks, leaving Gamaliel free again to go down to the pond every day, and stand there staring across the ice toward the falls, in peace.

From behind the wall, I watched him, as he stood squinting out into the gray afternoon, through the snow-fog rising from the pasture. Twice, three times, I saw him venture out onto the pond. Deliberately, as if courting danger.

I knew his sensation, as he struggled to keep his footing, walking on frozen water, faced with the fear and the attraction of the falls, suddenly fluid at the edge of the ice.

What was he thinking? I wondered. That he could find his father there?

But even I had begun to think that the strange landscape painter could not be his father. Gamaliel should have a better father than that.

"They ought to lock him in the looney bin," scowled Henry, arriving at my side with Peter, rubbing a finger across the fresh scar on his head.

"Uncle Tim should put him in jail," insisted my brother Jake, tossing a rotted apple at Peter's back.

"Your Uncle Tim couldn't put a chicken in jail," scoffed Peter, giving Jake a punch.

"Pick on someone your own size," I hollered, giving Peter a shove.

Tim's boys rose to defend their father, and Henry took two of them on at a time, and suddenly we were all fighting, which left our beleaguered mothers angry enough to leave the lot of us, black eyes and all, locked away in the woodshed until we made up.

For weeks our mothers had been baking, the breads and cakes and pies for the family Christmas Eve Feast in the old stone house on Howeside Farm, when all descendants of Ephraim and Rebecca Howe still in residence in Old Bell Falls would crowd in to eat and make merry and celebrate my father's birthday, before going off to hear Uncle Gideon preach.

I wondered, locked up in the shed with Henry and Peter and Nate and the rest, my mouth watering from the baking smells, whether our mothers were thinking about the big empty place at Meadside. Wasted on two people, while they must cram about a hundred of us into Ephraim Howe's old stone house.

And I found myself wondering once again why a family of carpenters hadn't bothered to make more than just a few incidental additions to the ancestral home, in view of the mansion (bigger than our place by sixteen huge rooms!) on the other side of the pond.

"Just letting the air stay outside," my father would say, if anyone made the suggestion. Whatever he meant by that. Or "We have all we need," which is what he always said about everything.

Let out of our woodshed prison at last, we Howe boys reveled in Christmas Eve. Due to the size of the family, most of us between the ages of eight and eighteen (all the boys, and most of the girls) spent the afternoon and evening outside, around the huge bonfire in the yard, or carousing in the barn, swinging on the rope, diving from the loft into fresh hay, warmed by the presence of beasts.

Along about six o'clock, coming in from the barn for some more fruitcake and hot cider, we witnessed a most startling event.

We were accustomed to Grandfather Luther, sitting upright in his chair, mechanically rocking, staring blankly into the fire, wrapped in the old quilt his mother Rebecca had made for him when he was a child. (So attached was he to this tattered piece of patchwork, that my mother, in order to wash it, must pry it from his hands as he slept.)

We were accustomed to Luther's silence, broken only, from time to time, by a sudden dark moan, as if he suffered a pain too deep for words.

But tonight, it was as if he suddenly woke to another state, making a strange high sound, like the voice of an injured child. And then, he spoke!

"Go back, Mother!" he cried, as clear as day. "Go back for the boy!" And he slumped back into his wide-eyed, stroke-sound sleep.

Father's face was troubled after that, and Mother watched him with care.

Along about seven o'clock the kinsfolk began to take leave, until only the family of Hannah and Luther remained—my fatherr's brothers and sisters and their families (still a crowd, but one the house could hold), to celebrate my father's birthday.

At my mother's summons, all the children gathered at the foot of the Christmas Tree, a fresh-cut fir we had dragged down only that morning from above the high pasture (careful as always to choose a specimen from our side of an imaginary extension of Ephraim's wall).

My father, I thought, was unusually sober as he received the congratulations and hearty backslapping of his brothers (a *Farmer's Almanac* from Uncle Tim, a collection of religious meditations from Uncle Gideon), the fussing of his sisters (their knitted socks and scarves, Aunt Mildred's traditional garish wool cap), the adoration of nieces and nephews, until at last it was our turn.

"James, go fetch your father's gift," my mother said.

Each of us children who was hold enough had contributed a quarter from our chore money, and Mother had ordered our gift special through the General Store. It was a pleasure to see Father, having pulled off the careful wrappings, lift the lid of the cardboard box and delight at our gift—a shiny silver fountain pen with three extra points, a box of snow-white cotton bond paper, and a pot of India ink.

"Why, William!" exclaimed Aunt Meg. "Just as when Grandmother was alive!"

"Yes, I remember," joined Aunt Millie. "Only then it was those leather notebooks you used to write in. The ones you kept in that old tin box."

"Yes," remembered Meg. "Whatever happened to your pretty box, William?"

Simultaneously, Uncles Tim and Gideon cleared their throats and stood.

"Well," they said together, each pulling out a pocket watch.

"It's late," said Constable Tim.

"Yes, indeed," agreed The Reverend Gideon. "Time I was off to the church," he smiled. "Where I shall no doubt see every one of you very soon!"

An hour later, everyone had bustled off to the service, leaving half a dozen little ones with my mother, who in any event was remaining behind this year, on account of our new baby sister, and to tend Grandfather Luther, of course.

My father, in no hurry to depart, moved away (with an indulgent smile) from the usual disputations over which among us children was old enough to benefit from Uncle Gideon's Christmas message and which would be more profitably left behind. Susannah thought she should stay behind to help Mother, and was allowed.

We stood apart from the others, Susannah and I, watching our father, thoughtful, pass by Old Luther at the fire, lay a hand for a moment on his shoulder, as if to give comfort, and then move on, carrying his birthday gift into the "library" at the back of the house.

"You best stay out of mischief tonight, James," Susannah said, her gray eyes, sober, upon me. "There's a storm coming."

"I know," I said, and I would have attempted a denial of her implication, but for the interruption.

"The baby is crying, Susannah!" our mother called, occupied with Aunt Faith's two-year-old twins. And my sister was off to rescue Baby Tess from the cradle, leaving me alone to pursue my interest in our father's behavior.

Through the open door to the small, cramped

room at the rear of the house, I saw him sit in his hand-crafted captain's chair and lift the top of his massive oak desk, the mysteriously jointed wood rolling back, disappearing like magic to disclose the working space.

Deliberately, he laid the cardboard box on the desktop and took out the sheaf of snow-white paper. Careful not to damage a single sheet, he deposited the sheaf in a wooden tray of exactly the right size. (He had made them all with his own hands—the chair, the desk, and the wooden tray.)

Next, he lifted out the pot of India ink, which fit perfectly into the ink well to his right. Then he placed the pen points in a small drawer above the ink, and took up the silver pen itself, which he held, rolling it between fingers and thumb.

In a moment, he sighed, and, laying the pen beside the ink well, he reached back under the row of pigeon holes along the top of the desk to pull out the box, shining tin in a patterned mosaic, dented, but still bright, and tied with heavy string.

Untying the string, he lifted the lid, and then laid it to one side. Briefly, he laid his right hand flat upon whatever was inside, and then he lifted out a leather book, and opened it to the end.

He read for a moment and then, giving a deep sigh, he closed the book, turning to look at me, as if knowing I had been watching him all the while.

"What is it, Father?" I dared.

"A charge from my grandmother, son. Something I have too long neglected."

I was afraid of this notion that my father could be in any way flawed.

"Come, James," he said, replacing the book, and closing the bright tin box. "It's time to go to church."

Victory

We come at last to the part of the story with which I began. Christmas Eve, nineteen thirty-three.

While our elders listened to Uncle Gideon, and sang carols on Birchwood Hill, my cousins and brother Jacob and I sneaked away to find Gamaliel at the pond.

We seized the moment, as Uncle Gideon, arms lifted in praise, lifted his eyes as well, addressing heaven (or at least the rafters) with the voice of gladness:

"For the comforts, dear friends, of our prosperous associations, one with another, in this, our beloved time-honored peaceful habitation . . . " By the time he took a breath and dropped his eyes again to the congregation, we had slipped from the back row, and were gone.

Let boys be boys, they might have thought to one another—the parents and aunts, uncles, great-uncles, and such—had they noticed we were gone.

Under the baritone ripple of Uncle Gideon's Christmas Eve admonitions, we moved away from the warm, glowing church and slipped down Birchwood Hill. As the voice rose to the fevered pitch of its sermonal ecstasy ("Let us rejoice!"), we tramped a path through deep snow, making a shortcut to the bridge.

Under the fading strains of the choir *("It came u- pon a midnight clear . . ."),* we crossed over to Meadside. As the congregation joined *("Peace on the ea-rth, good will to men!"),* we began our trek across the frozen fields up past the falls to Abnak Pond.

Sure enough, he was there, a gray shadow, alone in the cloudy moonlight, staring out over the ice as the snow began to fall. (How could I defend him with a dozen Howes bent upon his torment!)

Silent, we slid among birches, slipped among willows, faces whipped and stinging.

My heart thudding in my chest, I waited, watching Gamaliel, alone in the gathering storm.

And then, it began.

An eerie call floated into the night. "Wooooo! Woo-ooo!" wailed Henry from deep in the dark birch grove.

Gamaliel cocked his head, listening, black eyes peering into the thickening swirl of snow.

"Wooooo! Saaave meeeee!" Henry moaned.

Nate was in the willows: "Gamaayylee-el! It is yoou! The choooosen one!"

Pete was farther up, crying downwind: "Lift the curse, Gamaylee-el! Saaave me!"

At the edge of the pond Gamaliel turned, as if searching for the sounds.

Slipping through the willows, they tormented him, calling, wailing, throwing stones out onto the ice to confuse him.

"Saave meeeee, Gamaliel! It is I-I-I-I-I! Marguerite LaPoinnnte!"

"Help meeee! Gamaaaaaylielllllll! Saaaave meeee!"

He turned faster now, abrupt, afraid, a phantom in the snow, turning and turning at the voices.

Tense, poised for rescue, I watched, sensing his loss of direction.

"Gamaliel!" I cried, but it only frightened him more.

He moved now, a gray form obscuring in the storm, slipping down the bank in his confusion, sliding out onto the ice!

In the swirling, whistling snow, I could barely make him out, as he spun to get his bearings, slipping on the ice.

The wailing was the sound of hungry wolves, my cousins in frozen willows and ghostly birches, tormenting a helpless boy, struggling on the ice.

And the injustice of it overtook me.

"Stop!" I screamed. "He doesn't know the way!"

They didn't stop, only increased their howling, the sounds whipping 'round with the wind.

Through the storm I saw Gamaliel scrambling on the ice, desperate for safety, but moving fast . . . in the wrong direction!

Gradually, their howling had faded, and I knew that they had wearied of the game, grown too cold, and were gone.

But too late! Blinded, deafened by the assault of fear and snow, Gamaliel was moving out toward the thinning ice, and the rocky, treacherous falls!

"Stop!" I screamed, running, falling, sliding down the bank until my feet struck the hard slick surface of the pond.

"Gamaliel! Stop!" I cried, my voice whirling back upon me in the wind, as if I cried in silence.

In a frenzy, I crawled along the ice, clawed my way through frozen willows, frantic to keep abreast of him, to reach him before it was too late.

When I heard the crack, I froze.

As if in awful sympathy, the storm winds ceased, and in the sudden silence, I felt, then heard, the deeper, more terrifying sound of the falls.

"Gamaliel!" I screamed.

The winds resumed, fury increasing, and I saw him, a gray shadow falling, slipping from sight.

Ripping off my scarf, I thrust myself forward, making a dive on my belly across the ice, crushing my lungs, stopping far short of the desperate shadow thrashing in black water at the edge of the ice.

Gasping for breath, I crept toward him, reaching. "Gamaliel!" I gasped, throwing out my scarf. "Over here!" But the sounds of the storm and the falls drowned my voice.

Reckless, I spun 'round, sliding on my back, feet first, toward Gamaliel clinging to the edge of the ice. Bracing on my elbows, I slid, the freezing water rising up past my boots, to my knees. The water rising to my waist, I pushed my thoughts out toward him, made a picture of him in my brain, grabbing my boots, holding fast. I imagined his relief, willed into myself the strength I would need to pull us both to safety.

My brain flooded with imaginings, with the sounds of storm and raging water, I felt the CRACK! Felt it under my back, and down to my feet. And, lifting my head in horror, I saw that he was gone!

In that instant, I knew that I must save myself, to have any hope of saving him. Soaked now to my shoulders, I flipped over, crawling in a frenzy for the bank, my wet clothes weighing me like lead, the ice cracking fast behind me.

A frozen blade in my chest, I swam through ice and snow, to the shore, up the bank, swam in a nightmare of swirling snow through the birch grove, across the bridge, and up the hill, screaming for help.

"Silent Night, Holy Night, sleep in heavenly peace," they were singing, deaf to my wind-wrapped cries.

Then, unaware of how I traveled, I was under the tower, as the bells pealed the end of the Christmas Eve service, the sound ringing in my frozen bones.

"Help!" I choked, bursting breathless through the heavy doors. "He's in the pond!"

"Who?!" they cried, moving as one to the rescue. "Who is it, boy?" they cried, not stopping for a reply, lanterns appearing from nowhere, to split the white-dark night.

"We'll never find him!" a mother cried, once again counting her own.

"He'll be caught at the falls!"

"If he's not washed down!"

"If we can make it in time!"

Under the tower, the sexton began the toll of alarm.

~

They found him wedged in a ragged outcrop on the Mead side of the center falls, risking their lives to save him, lashing themselves to the rope, a human chain fighting the freezing current and the slippery rocks, my father in the lead.

A shout went up as my father reached him, bracing himself in the icy stream, to lift him free. Another shout as my father laid him, limp, across his shoulder, and turned to make the journey back.

I watched, wrapped in Uncle Gideon's coat, forcing my lungs to taken in frozen air, my clothes like a shroud of ice, weighing my limbs. I watched, as in a dream, scarcely knowing how I had come to this place, as the line of men, Uncle Tim and Uncle Gideon nearest Father on the rope, fought the water and the storm, pulled with their might to hold him steady across the most treacherous point, where the current burst free to plunge over the ledge into the bottomless pool below.

And then, in an awful moment, they were gone, Father and his burden, footing lost on the rocks, slipping into the black water, disappearing from view, as Tim and Gideon and the others slid forward under the weight.

The shrieking all around me, every man and youth

running for the rope, I felt a gentle weight across my shoulders, over my head—my mother, arriving from Howeside, wrapping me in a quilt.

Struggling to find their feet, Tim and Gideon held fast to the rope, all of Old Bell Falls behind them, pulling, hauling, shouting into the wind, no possibility of surrender.

While on the bank, I stood frozen in swirling snow beside my mother, and prayed.

And then, the mightiest shout of all, as my father reappeared from the depths, tossing his head clear of the frigid water, grasping for a finger hold on slippery rock.

"Thank God!" my mother prayed as my father, the boy still secure on his back, was pulled from the deep.

"I heard it was you gave the warning, James," my mother said, choking back a sob. "You have saved his life."

Shaking to my core, tears freezing on my cheeks, I prayed that it would be so.

I watched them pull my father and his fearsome burden onto the bank, stripping off their coats to wrap them.

Held fast at my mother's side, I watched my father fall to his knees, lay Gamaliel on a bed of coats, townsfolk rushing forward with blankets. My heart bursting, I watched my father commence to work him, pushing his chest, while others rubbed his rigid, stone-cold hands.

"It's no use," I heard someone say. "He's gone."

NO! I cried in my mind. And I broke away, fighting through the crowd to stand beside my father, as he worked to bring Gamaliel back to life.

An eternity he worked, the townsfolk huddling around, protection from the storm.

Until, quiet, my father fell back.

"Somebody better fetch Victoria," said Uncle Tim. "There's nothing more we can do."

But before they could fetch her, she came running, wild down the hill through the foot-deep snow. Wild like the winter wind, breath sent out hard before her, with a wail like a crack in the earth.

"NO-O-O-O!"

White gown whipping in the storm, head and hands bare, she ran straight to him without a guide, ripping through the huddling folk like they were paper, ice tears on her cheeks.

"NO!" she cried. And again, "NO!"

Thrusting them from him, she fell to her knees, seized his hand in the sudden hush. Even the wind laid down its fury.

And then, she called him back. "Gamaliel!"

At his feet, I watched, as the spirit passed over him at the call, the color coming into his cheeks.

"Gamaliel!" she commanded.

All around me, I heard the gasp of the congregation, like one newborn's desperate breath, heard the wonder at the movement of his frozen eyes, the flood of water pouring warm from his lungs.

My heart broken, I fell to my knees beside my weeping father, while, weeping, my mother wrapped Victoria in her cloak.

Under the clearing sky, the weeping spread through the congregation, as Victoria, still kneeling in snow, raised her son to her heart.

For a moment, there was only weeping, and the toll of the warning bell. Until the message reached the church on Birchwood Hill, and the Christmas peal resumed: Peace, good will toward men.

~

Just before dawn, shivering in my bed, I saw my father, standing at my door.

"I can't get warm," I told him, whispering, so as not to awaken my brothers.

"I know, son," he said, and he was shivering, too. "Come. Let us take Old Luther to the fire."

A lifelong habit his failing mind could not alter, Grandfather had risen just before dawn. We found him standing, nowhere to go, seeing nothing, in the darkness of his room.

Without protest, he let us lead him, slowly, down the hall (past the room where Victoria Mead had fallen asleep, keeping vigil over her son), slowly to his chair. I wrapped him warm in Rebecca's old quilt, while my father stoked the fire.

Presently, the fresh logs caught, and the flames were leaping, flickering shadows across my father's hands and face. The heat from the fire reached my skin, and I was aware of my cold bones.

My father turned to warm his back, motioning me into his arms. We stood there locked, silent, no words for what we felt. My head against his chest, I listened to his heart.

Dawn was breaking. In the yard, the cock crowed. In the barn, the cattle stirred. Soft light touched the eastern window. The fir tree, dressed with tinsel and wooden angels, was a massive shadow in the corner of the room.

I was warm now, and my father released me. The logs on the fire crackled, sending an ember onto the hearth. My father stooped, and with his bare hand returned the ember to the grate.

In his chair, Old Luther stirred, turning his face toward the coming light.

The first rays streamed through the window, flooding the braided rug in the center of the smooth oak floor, the light growing, at each point touching upon something a Howe had made: The long oak table, the maple chairs, a knotted shawl draped over the horse-hair sofa, an embroidered linen cloth. On the fir tree, the tinsel sparkled.

In the growing light, my father knelt, gentle, at his father's side, a strong arm around his father's shoulders, a hand upon his father's knee.

"Christmas day, Father," he whispered.

No movement, but a change in my grandfather's face, as if, suddenly, he knew we were there. In the firelight, his old eyes glistened, a message from his captive soul. "Mother," was all he said.

Strength leaving, my grandfather slackened.

Weeping, I laid my hand upon my father's shoulder, as, weeping, he lifted his father's hand in his.

"Tell her . . ." my father tried, watching the glistening eyes close. "Tell her, " he said, his eyes upon the quiet face, ". . . it is finished."

And Old Luther, the patchwork falling from his shoulder, drew a last breath, and was still.

The sun rose bright in the clear blue sky over dazzling Old Bell Falls. The town awoke to the utter stillness of winter morning, the vast expanse clothing the landscape in white, so that no spot remained upon the earth. No stain. No mark of strife. From the border of the woods above the high pasture, down to the edge of Abnak Pond, the wall was the merest ripple in the virgin snow.

In a moment the church bells would begin to sound, ringing in Christmas Day. For the first time in nearly a hundred years, the bells, forged by Howe and Mead, would greet a town without division, from their tower on Birchwood Hill.

Fortunate we are when we are marked in youth by truth. Such a fortunate one was I, when I saw a holy season redeemed by the healing of hearts.